TRINOYONI

Moitrayee Bhaduri is an author, screenwriter and content specialist. Her first book, *The Sinister Silence* (2015), introduced the feisty private detective Mili Ray. Her mini-thriller series on Inspector K.P. Singh (2020–21) has been optioned for screen adaptation. Moitrayee has a background in writing and communications and has worked in the IT sector for many years. She completed her bachelor's in history with honours from Loreto College and her master's from Jadavpur University, Kolkata. She also has a certificate in creative writing from the University of Oxford. A dog lover and coffee-addict, Moitrayee enjoys reading, singing and solving crosswords.

You can reach her at moitrayeebhaduri@gmail.com.

TRINOYONI
THE SLAUGHTERER OF SONAGACHI

MOITRAYEE BHADURI

Published by
Rupa Publications India Pvt. Ltd 2022
7/16, Ansari Road, Daryaganj
New Delhi 110002

Sales centres:
Allahabad Bengaluru Chennai
Hyderabad Jaipur Kathmandu
Kolkata Mumbai

Copyright © Moitrayee Bhaduri 2022

This is a work of fiction. All situations, incidents, dialogue and characters, with the exception of some well-known historical and public figures mentioned in this novel, are products of the author's imagination and are not to be construed as real. They are not intended to depict actual events or people or to change the entirely fictional nature of the work. In all other respects, any resemblance to persons living or dead is entirely coincidental.

All rights reserved.
No part of this publication may be reproduced, transmitted, or stored in a retrieval system, in any form or by any means, electronic, mechanical, photocopying, recording or otherwise, without the prior permission of the publisher.

P-ISBN: 978-93-5520-865-1
E-ISBN: 978-93-5520-866-8

First impression 2022

10 9 8 7 6 5 4 3 2 1

The moral right of the author has been asserted.

Printed in India

This book is sold subject to the condition that it shall not, by way of trade or otherwise, be lent, resold, hired out, or otherwise circulated, without the publisher's prior consent, in any form of binding or cover other than that in which it is published.

*In fond remembrance of my dearest college professor,
Mrs Shreela Roy, who inspired me to love history and
write books.
In loving memory of my braveheart friends—
Shamim Dicholkar, Vishal Das, Vidyaranya Kollipal and
Sweta Sengupta—who left the world a bit too soon.*

Contents

Author's Note	ix
Early Life	1
Four Years Later	7
Tara Debi	11
The Inseparable Bond	16
The Young Widow	20
Prabhat Babu	24
The Couple Elopes to Calcutta	28
A New Chapter in Trina's Life	30
Life in Sonagachi	38
The Transformation	44
The Rise of the Courtesan	49
Ram Babu	56
Manik	64
The Dangerous Duo's First Victim	74

Crimes Surrounding Marriage	82
The Fake Wedding	89
The Infamous Kidnappings	99
The Daring Daroga	107
The Daroga Meets the Fraudster Duo	118
The Daroga in Pursuit	124
Life after Ram Babu	143
The Spiritual Guru	146
The Serial Killer's First Prey	157
Murder or Suicide?	164
A Close Shave	170
The Return of Daroga Sukumar	179
Rajlakshmi's Mysterious Death	185
Trapping the Serial Killer	201
The Execution	217
Afterword	221
Further Reading and References	224
Glossary	225
Acknowledgements	229

Author's Note

This book is based on the true story of Troilokya Tarini Debi, a fraudster and serial killer who robbed and murdered several women in Calcutta in the late nineteenth century. This is a dramatized account of the life and times of Troilokya, arguably the first female serial killer of India. Names of most of the characters have been changed and several fictional characters have been added, according to the demands of the manuscript. Several incidents and events in this book are fictional and have been included to dramatize the scenes narrated. The author has no intention to disrespect, impair or hurt the sentiments of any person(s), communities, religions or nationalities in this book.

Early Life

On a scorching summer noon in 1853, a tired Priyogopal Sanyal entered Purnendu Shekhar Chattopadhyay's house, wearing an irritated look. The 50-year-old Sanyal had travelled a long distance and could barely sit straight. His drowsy eyes and half-broken walking stick made him look much older than his age. He was chewing on a betel leaf and behaving rudely with his hosts.

People crowded around the house, inquisitive to learn about the man who would be marrying the prettiest girl in the village. Trina managed to catch a glimpse of the man and felt disgusted. She was appalled and couldn't understand why God had chosen this tragic destiny for her.

'Jamai babu was bedridden for two years because of a life-threatening disease,' Trina overheard her neighbour saying.

'Even in his bedridden state, he married four girls and rescued them,' Priyogopal Sanyal's friend, who had accompanied him, informed Purnendu.

With folded hands and a lowered head, Purnendu Chattopadhyay said, 'Our daughter is very sensible and compromising. She excels at all household chores. She will not give you any reason to complain. I am grateful to Sanyal babu for rescuing her and agreeing to marry her.'

Tears trickled down Trina's eyes as she saw her father begging Sanyal.

'Priyo babu has rescued ten other girls too. But your daughter is much older than his other wives,' Sanyal's friend remarked scornfully.

Purnendu looked at the groom apologetically and pleaded, 'I am an unfortunate father, burdened with the liability of an unmarried daughter. But as a Kulin Brahmin, I couldn't commit a sin by marrying her off to a non-Kulin gentleman! Please forgive me.'

Priyogopal Sanyal looked at Purnendu and nodded dismissively.

Sanyal's friend added, 'Priyo babu will accept the dowry and marry your daughter tomorrow. He will leave for East Bengal soon after to see his newborn son. Your daughter can continue living with you for now. You can complete the remaining rituals during his next visit.'

Purnendu nodded with folded hands and said, 'We are truly blessed to have found him.'

Trinoyoni Debi was born on a stormy Durga Ashtami night in 1840, in a tiny village in Bengal's Burdwan district while her father was organizing the auspicious weapon worship known as Astra Puja in the village temple. Purnendu Shekhar Chattopadhyay, a poor Brahmin priest, and his wife Sarala Debi named their daughter after the Goddess.

The whole village believed that Trinoyoni, endearingly

known as Trina, was the Goddess reincarnated and were captivated by her beauty. They crowded Purnendu's dilapidated hut to catch a glimpse of the angel-faced Trina. Purnendu decided to turn the situation to his advantage and placed a donation box near little Trina's feet, where visitors could deposit money after seeing Trina. With the collections from his daughter's 'darshan', Purnendu barely managed to make ends meet.

By the time Trina was three, she had begun to enjoy the attention she received from people. And by age ten, she was famous in her village as the *dana kata pori*.

Like other girls her age, Trina was an expert in household chores. Though she was inquisitive about books, she wasn't allowed to touch them. She was proud of her looks and confident that she would get married to the best-looking man in Burdwan. But, soon, her beauty became a cause of concern for her parents, and they found it difficult to shield her from evil eyes. Men of all ages would queue up outside Purnendu's house expressing their willingness to marry Trina. Suitors from many rich families approached Purnendu Chattopadhyay, but he rejected all the marriage proposals. Trina belonged to a Kulin Brahmin family—the highest rung in the Brahmin hierarchy—and though many prospective grooms were Brahmins, Purnendu was only looking for a pure Kulin Brahmin. As a result, even though it was normal for girls in the nineteenth century to be married off before they turned ten, Trina remained unmarried even at the age of twelve. As Trina turned thirteen, relatives expressed concern about her unmarried status, and the elders reminded Purnendu of the unwritten rules that every villager must abide by.

'It is a crime to keep a grown-up, unmarried daughter at home. My daughter is younger than Trina and is already expecting her second child. What are you waiting for, purohit mohashoy?' a village elder asked.

'But getting her married to anyone who is not Kulin will be a sin. The Gods will never forgive me and I will not find a place even in hell,' Purnendu explained.

'Why don't you look eastwards? There are many Kulin Brahmins there who are willing to marry and rescue our girls,' another elder commented.

'Besides, all that matters is his caste. His age, looks, economic and social status are irrelevant; a man is a man. A girl cannot remain unmarried for so long!'

These suggestions, with undertones of a threat, alarmed Purnendu. He knew that he had to marry his daughter off, even if that meant tying her to an elderly man on his deathbed. He was worried that if he delayed any further, he would deprive himself of the most noble duty of kanyadaan. Purnendu's relentless search for a groom for his daughter took him to East Bengal. After struggling for days, when he was packing his bags to return home, someone told him about Priyogopal Sanyal, an elderly man who was a Barendra Brahmin, considered as the highest subcaste among Kulin Bengali Brahmins.

∞

The next day, Trina was married to Priyogopal Sanyal and became his eleventh wife. The elderly groom kept coughing all through the rituals and fell asleep during the garland-exchange ceremony. His friends helped him place the garland around Trina's neck.

Trina let her tears flow freely. She wasn't allowed to raise even a faint voice of protest.

On the *phool shojya* with her husband, Trina looked like a princess in her bright red sari and gold jewellery. Her bedroom had been beautifully adorned with fragrant flowers. She sat petrified on the bed with the veil covering her face. Every time someone entered the room, her heart skipped a beat.

Almost two hours later, when thirteen-year-old Trina was sleepy, her fifty-year-old husband entered the room in an inebriated state. He lifted her veil and smirked. Trina was numb with fear. As Priyo tried to kiss her, Trina closed her eyes tightly and held her breath. She felt the strong smell of alcohol on his breath and sat clutching the covers, dreading the worst. But nothing happened. Trina waited, sweating in fear. Finally, she heard a faint sound and opened her eyes slowly. Her husband's head was on her pillow, and he was snoring away. She stared at him in disbelief.

And then, suddenly, she burst into childlike laughter. Tears trickled down her cheeks, but she couldn't stop laughing.

The next morning, the entire village gathered in front of Purnendu Chattopadhyay's house to catch a last glimpse of the village's new son-in-law before he departed. On his way out, Priyogopal accepted his dowry from Purnendu and bid hasty goodbyes.

After he left, Trina ran back into the house and pulled out her jewellery box. She couldn't stop admiring her new necklace and gold bangles. She was delighted to finally have her own gold jewellery, even though it had come at the cost of being married to Sanyal.

Four Years Later

Trina's husband, Priyogopal, had not returned to Burdwan to see his new wife since their wedding day. While Trina's father continued sending money to Priyogopal at regular intervals for four years, the family kept waiting for their son-in-law to visit and hoped that he would take Trina to East Bengal along with him.

Over the years, it had gotten increasingly difficult for Purnendu to meet Priyagopal's never-ending dowry demands. Trina's only joy since her wedding—the jewellery she owned— also had to be sold off. She cried uncontrollably, knowing that she was losing the only reward she had received for marrying a despicable man like Priyagopal. But she did not resist when her family had to sell her precious treasure. To add to the misery, Purnendu fell ill and was unable to continue working as a priest. When his meagre income also stopped, the savings started drying up and the family could barely manage to fend for themselves. While Trina's elder brother Shankar tried working as a priest to make ends meet, the increase in police vigilance following the sepoy mutiny of 1857 made it nearly impossible to go out in search of work without being held up by the police. So, the family gradually slid into destitution.

When Priyogopal stopped receiving money from Purnendu, he reached Trina's village. He misbehaved with her parents and berated them, demanding to know why they had stopped sending him the dowry money. Purnendu assured him that the money would reach him soon and pleaded with Priyogopal to take his daughter to her in-laws' home. But Priyogopal declined. When the parents begged, he insisted on spending the night with Trina before making a decision.

Everyone searched for Trina frantically all around the village but she was nowhere to be found. An angry Priyogopal walked out of Trina's house the next morning. He informed a pleading Purnendu that a fallen woman like Trina was unwelcome in his house.

Soon after Priyogopal's departure, Trina's parents learnt that she had been hiding at their neighbour, Tara Debi's house. They dragged Trina out of Tara's house, hurling abuses at her. Her mother screamed at her and slapped her while the whole village watched.

Trina felt humiliated. That evening, she sneaked out of her house and ran to the nearby pond. Her hands folded in prayer, she called out to the Goddess, 'Forgive me, Ma Durga! I have no other option.' Trina jumped into the water. Suddenly, she felt someone pulling her out. She tried to resist but fell unconscious. When she opened her eyes, she found herself lying in Tara's bed. Tara was sitting by her side, gently stroking her hair and drying her off so she wouldn't catch a cold.

Seeing her, Trina broke down in tears. 'Why did you save me, Tara didi? I don't want to live.'

'Just sleep now and never say such horrible things again,' Tara comforted Trina.

Trina kept looking at Tara, wondering if she was an angel in disguise.

'You don't have to return to your parents' house. You can live here as long as you want.' Tara assured Trina. Now that she was dry and had recovered, she dreaded heading back home to her family.

'But why, Tara didi?'

'I am your elder sister, that's why!' Tara replied, hugging Trina.

'But what if my husband returns and takes me away from you?' Trina asked innocently.

'Nobody can take you away from me,' Tara said, assertively.

Trina heaved a sigh of relief and put the fear of having to face her parents aside. Over the next few days, she grew extremely fond of Tara. Her life revolved around the Vaishnavite woman now. She continued to live in Tara's house, providing her companionship while Tara doted on and pampered Trina.

A couple of months later, news reached Trina from East Bengal that her husband was dead. Trina was scared about the painful rituals and customs that she would have to follow as a widow. The family would shave her head, forbid her from dressing up and force her to only wear white sarees. She would be denied her favourite food, spend almost half her life fasting and be asked to move out of the house and take shelter in a cowshed.

However, fate had something else in store for Trina.

'I have talked to your parents,' announced Tara. 'You don't have to observe the rigorous customs that widows follow. You can continue to live the way you want.'

'Really?' Trina jumped with joy and hugged Tara. 'Thank you, thank you,' she was ecstatic.

It was curious how Tara had convinced Trina's conservative father to let her be and not force her into a life of widowhood—her family didn't even ask her to get rid of her trousseau or shave her head. There were no restrictions on what she ate or wore. There was no difference between the married and the widowed Trina; a freedom that was unheard of in nineteenth-century Bengal.

Though Trina had moved back home, her proximity to Tara continued to grow after her husband's death. They spent hours together and Trina found a confidant in Tara. Their bond was such that Tara would grow restless if she didn't meet Trina every day, her love and kindness knew no bounds, and Trina was completely mesmerized by her.

Tara Debi

Tara did not like being confined to her house, and Trina became her companion to religious sites such as famous temples and to weekly haats (fairs), where people from different walks of life collected for commercial and entertainment purposes. At these weekly fairs, children would crowd the toy stalls and young women would rush to the imitation jewellery stalls.

Whenever eighteen-year-old Trina attended these fairs, she would be the cynosure of all eyes and the lustful gaze of men would make her uncomfortable. When she shared her concern, Tara simply laughed.

During one such fair in the village, Trina spotted a man trying to sell bangles to Tara, who never wore any jewellery apart from the flowers she sometimes tucked in her hair. So, Trina was rather surprised to witness the bangle-seller holding Tara's hand and trying to fit a bunch of bangles around her slender wrist. After watching them for a while, Trina realized that Tara wasn't wearing the bangles. The man was simply brushing his hand against Tara's and nudging her sari off with his elbow, grinning as he did so. Suddenly, Tara noticed Trina watching them.

'Do you want some bangles?' Tara asked. 'Come here.'

Trina shook her head but walked towards Tara. The Vaishnavite woman asked for a pair of bangles for the young widow, but as the man advanced towards Trina, she turned her back towards him and ran away.

When they returned home, Trina complained to Tara about the bangle-seller.

'I didn't like that man, didi,' Trina expressed. 'Why were you talking to him so nicely?'

Tara smiled and replied, 'He was a man in distress, Trina. He received solace when I touched him. It is my duty as a servant of God to help humankind in any way possible.'

'But—'

'Men have needs, Trina. And it is our duty, as women, to satiate their urges. We have come to this world to fulfil their desires and give them what they want.'

'But what will I get in return?' Trina wondered.

'Money, food and security for as long as you want. If you take care of men well enough, you will always be able to live comfortably and peacefully.'

Trina listened attentively. While explaining the bangle-seller's needs to Trina, Tara didn't mention the coins that the man had slipped through Tara's sari down her neck, allowing his hand to subtly feel the softness of Tara's flesh under the off-white sari that covered her body.

◦∞◦

Fifty-year-old Tara Debi was a good-looking Vaishnavite woman whose origins were shrouded in mystery, but her now-fading beauty indicated that she had been quite a stunner in her heyday. Tara had migrated to the small village in Burdwan a decade ago and had mingled with the village community. She lived in a shanty straw hut, adjacent to Trina's parents' house. Everyone knew her to be a helpless Vaishnavite widow who begged for a living. Some villagers also assumed that Trina's Brahmin parents had given shelter to poor Tara.

Tara was the epitome of simplicity. Usually dressed in a milky-white starched saree with a garland of tulsi leaves around her neck, Tara wore earrings and a nose-pin made of fine beads and carried a small *botua*, containing religious necklaces that she used for her prayers. Like a true Vaishnavite, Tara generally began and ended her sentences with 'Hari Om' and 'Hari Bol'.

The earliest memory Trina had of Tara was of a pleasant-looking woman with a big sandalwood tika on her forehead, gently pushing the half-broken door of her straw house to venture out to the streets with a begging bowl in hand.

Once Trina's brother Shankar had expressed his dissatisfaction to Trina, 'You are always worshipping that fallen woman! Have you noticed that she doesn't go out to beg anymore? How is she arranging for food and money? Who provides for her?'

Scared of her brother, Trina had replied sheepishly, 'Oh...I have seen her begging.'

'Has anyone in the village even seen her husband?' her brother responded, furiously. 'We've only heard that he went missing from the village. Why didn't he ever return? She has no answer.'

Trina knew that her brother had spoken the truth. But she loved Tara too much to doubt her about anything.

Another time, as Shankar had left for the temple, Trina had seen her neighbour Dhuri babu and his wife walking home along with Tara, and had noticed a fish-knife in Tara's hand.

Dhuri babu had sounded grateful, 'Thank you, Tara! Had you not stopped me at the right time, I would have killed my wife today. I thought she was cheating on me.'

'You will never need to use this, Dhuri babu,' Tara had said, pointing at the fish-knife in her hand, 'your wife worships you.' The wife had smiled coyly. Dhuri babu had paid some money to Tara for her help, who had gracefully accepted the money with folded hands.

Trina had witnessed Tara helping people earlier also. Once, two women had been fighting over carrying water from the nearby pond, and Tara had intervened and solved the issue, leading to the fighting women finally embracing each other.

Tara could sense the pulse of the village. She always played a big role in the marriage ceremonies and festivals in the village. She would sing and bless married couples and attend their *bashor raat* celebrations too.

To this, Trina's mother had once remarked, 'That's how the greedy widow feeds herself!'

But Trina felt that Tara was kind to everyone because there was a void in her own life, which she filled through interacting with people and helping them. To her, Tara came across as a reliable and devout person who selflessly helped everyone she could. She had never met anyone, except her family, who had spoken ill of her Tara didi. She saw her as a as a simple Vaishnavite woman, who begged for a living and roamed around the village singing kirtans praising the Lord.

The Inseparable Bond

'We believe in the power of *kanthi-badal*,' Tara stated while massaging Trina's scalp with oil. The two were in Tara's hut, which had become a lot more comfortable after the roof had been repaired recently. Trina no longer felt like she was freezing whenever there was the slightest chance of wind or rain in the village.

'What is that, Tara didi?' Trina asked innocuously, sitting on the floor while Tara sat on the bed.

'Kanthi-badal is an age-old Vaishnavite practice where a couple gets married by simply exchanging a string of beads. A few months after abandoning me, my husband performed kanthi-badal with a woman in my neighbouring village. My in-laws abandoned me too, and I was homeless for a long time. I didn't know what to do. I looked for my husband everywhere but he was dead by then, I think!' exclaimed Tara. She dipped her fingers in oil again and continued massaging Trina's scalp.

'If you were not sure of his death, why did you embrace widowhood, Tara didi?' Trina asked. She often wondered how Tara spent her time at home when Trina wasn't there. Even though it was a small hut, she was sure Tara must get lonely, not having a family or anyone to call her own.

'You will understand when you grow up,' Tara said, skirting the question and started making pigtails with Trina's hair.

Then, she continued, 'After a few years, I met another man and we performed kanthi-badal. Later, that man also left me and exchanged kanthi with someone else, dissolving our marriage. But I didn't lose heart. Even today, if a man in distress needs me, I will do my best to fulfil his needs.'

'But is this kanthi-badal good for women?' asked Trina.

Tara responded, 'Of course! To save us from utter despair, the great Vaishnavite men started kanthi-badal so that widowed women like me can take shelter offered by another man. It is not a sin but a blessing.'

Saying this, the moist-eyed Tara hugged Trina.

Trina and Tara's conversations brought them closer than ever; in fact, they were inseparable. The moment Trina was free from her household chores, she would run to Tara's house. Tara doted on Trina like she was her own daughter. Along with her wonderful company and conversations, Trina really liked Tara's house. While, from the outside, Tara's hut looked more or less the same as Purnendu's home, the inside was starkly different and something, Trina was sure, only she had seen. There was more furniture in Tara's house than Trina's home.

Trina's family didn't like her close proximity to Tara. Shankar often scolded Trina for meeting Tara whenever she entered her home after having spent the day with the older woman. But nothing could tear Trina away from Tara.

One day, Shankar fell miserably ill and no *kobiraj*, or doctor, could cure him. After suffering for days, the young man breathed his last, leaving his family devastated. Trina and her parents were broken and overcome with grief. Tara was constantly by Trina's side during this time and tried to comfort her in the best way possible.

As Trina spent more time with Tara, she slowly started believing that a woman was incomplete without a man in her life. Tara started getting more involved in Trina's daily life. She bought her food, new clothes and occasionally gave her money to buy things for sheer indulgence too. Tara's hypnotic charm had cast a spell on Trina.

Tara offered help to Trina's parents too, who now had no money, no savings and no son who could go out and work. But, being rigid, conservative Brahmins, they refused to accept any help from Tara, a lower caste woman.

One day, Tara met the ailing Purnendu and said, 'Purohit mohashoy, I am a Vaishnavite woman fulfilling my moral duty and serving the dictums of my forefathers, who according to their "dharma" believed that they must help Brahmins in distress. Please allow this lesser mortal to be of some use to you. I humbly request you to accept whatever little I have earned through begging over the years. People in this village have been very kind and caring towards me. Please permit me to serve you.'

Trina's parents listened to Tara but didn't say anything.

She continued, 'If you don't want to accept any help from this poor Vaishnavite woman, I understand. After all, you are a upper caste Brahmin. However, you can always borrow money from me and return it later. What do you think?'

Finally, the Chattopadhyay family agreed to accept financial help from Tara on the condition that they would return it to her once their situation had improved.

Over the next few months, Trina's parents' health improved and their financial situation became stable. Their stance on Tara changed, and they reasoned that she was an extremely kind soul and a messenger of God.

Sarala Debi told her husband, 'After the demise of our son, Tara looks after us as if we are her family. I sometimes see my Shankar in her.' The two teared up at the memory of their departed son and remembered with shame how poorly they had treated Tara through the years.

The next day, Purnendu and Sarala Debi bowed their heads and apologized to Tara for their earlier misbehaviour.

Tara smiled and, with folded hands, said, 'Hari Bol! You are Brahmins. Never lower your heads before me. I am honoured to be able to serve you.'

The Young Widow

Soon, Tara was running Trina's family. They were indebted to her for all the financial and emotional support she had provided, and Trina was spending even more time with her.

Tara had been discussing love and loneliness with Trina at length. Trina didn't understand why, every day, Tara raised the same topic and continued applauding the men of the world. One evening, when it was raining heavily, Tara returned home earlier than usual and called Trina to her house. Trina happily followed, hoping to munch on the goodies she had seen in Tara's hand. Tara handed a sweet to Trina and said, 'You know Trina, a man can change your world and give you all the security that you desire.'

Trina didn't say anything and kept nibbling on the sweet.

'You can feast on such sweets every day if you meet the right man,' she looked carefully at Trina, 'I want to introduce you to Prabhat babu. He is a wonderful person,' Tara continued cautiously.

Trina had heard Tara mention the word babu, or gentleman, earlier also, elucidating how a certain 'babu' can add sparkle to her shabby life. This babu wouldn't be a husband, but someone who would pamper her, dote on her and fulfil all her worldly desires.

Curious, Trina asked, 'Is this the same babu you have been talking about all of last week?'

'No,' replied Tara. 'This person is special.'

Tara lovingly touched Trina's chin and played with a strand of her lustrous hair that refused to sit still on Trina's head and kept slipping over her eyes.

'See, I have already told you the advantages of having a babu in your life. He, too, will play with your hair the way I do, but you will derive a sea of pleasure when he does so. Besides, your life will be full of activity—you will dance, sing, play cards, enjoy a good meal together and feel your soul evolving from a girl's into a woman's,' Tara contended.

'But I am a Hindu Brahmin widow, Tara didi. How can I enjoy such forbidden pleasures?' asked Trina.

'Are you following the rituals that a Bengali Brahmin widow abides by?' laughed Tara.

Trina shook her head.

'If I tell you that you can survive without such rigid norms, you can. So, when I say that a young woman like you deserves to soak in the pleasure of physical and emotional intimacy, trust me,' said Tara. 'Men will enhance your happiness and you will never be poor again.'

The last line hit Trina instantly. 'Really? I will never be poor again if a man enters my life?' In her short experience so far, the converse had been true. She had been married to Priyogopal Sanyal for four years, which had led to nothing but her family growing poorer. She had lost her fine clothes and all her jewellery to pay dowry.

Tara grinned. 'Exactly! And, there is something more

enjoyable than money that a babu can give you.'

Trina's eyes sparkled with curiosity, 'What is that?' She saw the colour in Tara's eyes change and her pupils dilate.

Tara took a deep breath and started, 'You became a widow just after you reached puberty. Did your husband touch you?'

'Eeks! No,' Trina shuddered at the thought of the old and wrinkled Priyogopal touching her.

'You are a pure girl because no man has established any physical contact with you yet. Any man will want to have you and treat you like a queen! All you need to do is please him. You are so attractive that men will automatically get allured by your charm!'

'I don't understand,' Trina looked perplexed.

The weather outside was getting worse. The strong force of the cold winds threatened to damage Tara's straw hut. Trina curled up beside Tara in one corner of the hut to keep the rains from wetting her sari. She held Tara's hand tightly and shivered at the sound of thunder. Tara looked closely at Trina and gently removed Trina's sari, letting it fall on the ground. Shocked and embarrassed, Trina tried to hold on to the garment, but Tara held her firmly and ordered her to let it be. As Trina frantically tried to cover her body with her bare hands, Tara began touching Trina.

'What are you doing, Tara didi?' Trina's voice shivered with fear and cold.

'Shhh...think of me as a man,' Tara ordered.

'Oh,' eighteen-year-old Trina cringed while Tara touched her. She wanted to scream and move Tara's hand away, but as the older woman continued, Trina's resistance steadily faded.

'You have been missing the pleasure of pain from your life, my dear girl,' said Tara after she was done and helped drape the sari around Trina.

That night, sheltered from the rain in a rickety hut with Tara, Trina felt a new sensation in her body, something that she wasn't even aware existed.

Though Trina was taken aback by the suddenness of Tara's moves, she realized that something was missing from her life—a man to satiate her physical needs.

Trina couldn't get over the experience of that night. Tara continued to meet Trina and talk to her about the importance of having a man in her life.

However, Tara never touched Trina again.

Prabhat Babu

A month later, Tara inquired if Trina was ready to meet Prabhat *babu*, a charming young man she kept waxing lyrical about.

Apart from her horrendous tryst with Priyogopal years ago, Trina had never been so close to a man in her entire life. After the night where Tara had revealed to her the truth and magic of desire, Trina's excitement knew no bounds when she was introduced to Prabhat. Trina was shy, but her desperately pounding heart convinced her that she was meant to be with this man. She silently thanked God that her fate was not cursed after all.

In the first few meetings, Trina let Prabhat do all the talking. He had a small business of brokerage, and lots of interesting stories to share. Each meeting left Trina wanting to meet Prabhat again. Tara would arrange these secret meetings, and while Trina had no clue why Tara was taking so much interest in her love life and buying her new clothes and make-up to doll her up, she was so smitten by Prabhat that she did not bother to inquire.

With twenty-five-year-old Prabhat's entry into her life, Trina felt a sense of belonging. Unlike Tara, she was unaware of the details of Prabhat's actual business. Her beauty and naivety charmed Prabhat and, before he knew it, he had fell in love with Trina.

Trina shed all her inhibitions and shared her life story with Prabhat and found solace in the warmth of his company. She worshipped him, as he had given her hopes to dream about a life that she never knew existed—a life filled with happiness, luxury and peace.

Prabhat introduced Trina to different kinds of sensual pleasures, and the two became inseparable. Trina drowned in erotic bliss and made it her life's goal to please Prabhat in every way possible, eagerly learning everything he had to teach her about the body and desire.

Nobody was aware of Trina's secret liaison with Prabhat. The two fulfilled their intimate pleasures at Tara's house, who guarded their privacy with utmost tact. Even Trina's parents were unaware of the storm that had unsettled the coy village girl's heart.

Several months after Trina and Prabhat's secret affair began, Tara fell severely ill. Seeing the despair on Trina's face, Prabhat arranged for a doctor from the city to treat Tara. However, Trina learnt from the doctor that Tara was infected with a terminal disease. Within a few days, Tara's health deteriorated so much that she nearly lost her eyesight and requested Trina to stay by her side. Two weeks after she was diagnosed, Tara breathed her last in Trina's arms. Before dying, she had donated all her wealth and belongings to Trina's ailing parents.

In between coughing up blood and straining to speak, Tara had confessed, 'I may have sinned but I love Trina like my own sister. My earnest request is to you purohit mohashoy...please accept whatever little wealth I have and allow me to die peacefully. This is the highest honour for any soul on earth—to be of some use to Brahmins. Kindly allow me to die with peace in my heart.'

Even though Tara had been smiling on her deathbed, Trina had sensed that Tara's face reflected a deep sense of remorse, and she had wondered why Tara had been carrying guilt in her heart. Broken by the loss of her soul sister and companion, Trina fell apart after Tara's death. Prabhat tried to console her as best he could.

∞

After Tara's death, Trina and Prabhat found it extremely difficult to meet secretly.

One evening, Trina and Prabhat were caught red-handed in an intimate embrace at Tara's empty and now dilapidated house. Purnendu began shaking in anger and her mother fainted. The couple was embarrassed and scared. Purnendu threatened to kill Trina, even though he considered killing a Brahmin woman a grave sin.

Somehow, Trina and Prabhat managed to escape that night. The next morning, Prabhat learnt that the angry villagers were on their way to Trina's house, armed with fish-knives, bamboo sticks and other household items they could use as weapons. They had resolved to kill Trina and Prabhat. How could a Kulin Brahmin woman commit the heinous sin of indulging in an illicit affair with a married man? Prabhat's relatives also reached Burdwan and were looking for him.

Around this time, news reached Prabhat that the East India Company's rule in India was coming to an end. By the Queen's Proclamation, in November 1858, India came under the direct rule of the British government with Queen Victoria as its head. Prabhat decided to check with a friend if it would be wise to take Trina to Calcutta. Only after receiving confirmation did Prabhat leave for Calcutta with Trina. They hid all day among the swamps and the bushes. Finally, late at night, with the help of a villager who had accepted money in return for their safe passage, Prabhat and Trina eloped.

The Couple Elopes to Calcutta

Trina had never stepped out of her village before eloping with Prabhat. She was awestruck when she reached Calcutta. The smallest buildings in the city were much bigger than the temple in Burdwan, which was the largest structure there. She was spellbound at the size of the city and its neighbourhoods. She had never seen so many people together in her life. The bustling city life made her hopeful. 'I am finally going to live my life,' she thought.

As she walked alongside Prabhat, Trina noticed a rich man clad in dhoti-kurta walking with a woman wearing an expensive benarasi sari that was deep red and green. She had alta on her feet and her face was covered with the pallu of the sari. Trina noticed that her hands and neck were generously covered with gold jewellery and she was wearing *shakha pola nowa*. Behind the couple were two men carrying their luggage. Trina imagined herself as the newly wed bride, travelling with her young husband with a bag full of dreams. Her daydreaming was interrupted as Prabhat tapped her shoulder gently.

'Let's go. The carriage is waiting for us.'

Trina had seen carriages before, but she had never dreamt

of riding one. Prabhat helped her mount the horse-drawn carriage as the charioteer picked up the luggage.

Riding on the carriage like a queen, Trina was awestruck and kept turning her head from left to right in excitement, taking in all that she was witnessing. Big houses, beautiful horse-drawn carriages, women dressed differently and extravagantly, men wearing western clothes, food stalls and big markets, the vibrant city overflowing with life caught her fancy. Trina made a promise to herself: *I will make this city my home.*

When the carriage finally stopped and Trina alighted along with Prabhat, a big double-storey house stood tall before her. Trina followed Prabhat into the house and couldn't stop ogling at the women inside, admiring their taste in clothes. There she was, an eighteen-year-old widow, with her heart full of dreams, in a house at Sonagachi—the biggest red-light area in Calcutta.

A New Chapter in Trina's Life

As Trina entered the house, she saw something she would never forget for the rest of her life. Once she crossed the threshold and entered the house, she reached the *uthon* of the house. It looked like a *bonedibari*. There were rooms all around the courtyard—eight on the ground floor and nine on the upper floor. Most of the rooms were occupied by women who were freely mingling with each other and having a good time. Trina had never seen anything like this—neither such a big house nor women moving around so freely.

This place was markedly different from the village where Trina had grown up. There, women were in purdah and forbidden to leave their homes, unless permitted by the men. This was the first time that Trina had witnessed so many women occupying a house and not being instructed by a man on how they should conduct themselves! The women were beautifully dressed and had male servants and housemaids attending to them. Trina assumed that their husbands were kings, princes or zamindars who took such good care of their womenfolk.

She failed to understand which caste these women belonged to but was sure that they were all rich and well-fed.

They all looked similar and it was difficult to understand how the women were related to one another. The sound of chit-chat and laughter that had been missing from her life, reminded Trina of her childhood.

Prabhat led Trina into a vacant room in the house and smilingly said, 'This is going to be our residence from now. Nobody will disturb us here. You can do whatever you like.'

'Really?' Trina asked.

Prabhat nodded as an elderly lady entered the room. He greeted her with a smile.

'Trina, she is Rashmoni Debi, the owner of this house. You chat with her; I will be back in an hour or two.'

Rashmoni Debi was excessively fair, had long, lustrous hair and wore minimal jewellery. She was dressed in a classic *pacha pere* sari, procured from Kashi. She had a big tilak painted from her nose right up to the middle of her forehead, somewhat like Trina's Tara didi, and carried a botua with 'Hari Om' written all over it. She looked overtly religious.

Rashmoni Debi spoke gently and Trina instantly felt comfortable in her presence. They chatted for some time, after which other women of the house came forward to befriend her. Trina, who had been fascinated with gold since childhood, couldn't take her eyes off these women, all of whom sported ornate gold jewellery. They wore neatly ironed saris and had long, beautiful hair that most of them left open. Trina was amazed at their beauty and how well they maintained themselves. She was surprised to see some women nonchalantly smoking hookah, much like a zamindar. Their lifestyle, way of speaking and demeanour, all indicated that these were independent, strong women with a lot of wealth.

Trina became friendly with the group of women. All of them, except Sabita and Parama, were older than her. Trina began crying as she shared her life story with the women: her impoverished life, poor parents, her absconding husband and Tara didi's death.

Sabita wiped her tears and said, 'From today, you are our sister and friend too. I promise you that, in the days to come, you will also love, laugh and enjoy life like us. You will be independent and have the liberty to buy everything you like—fresh clothes, soaps, combs, sherbet, food of your choice—everything.'

The other women tried to cheer her up. They started advising Trina on how to do up her hair, how to apply snow powder and red colour on her lips, how to sexily chew on betel leaves and how to talk to men with confidence. Trina felt blessed to be in the company of these women.

As it was time for lunch, the women brought a big silver plate and served different kinds of food to Trina. She felt like a jamai, or son-in-law, never having experienced such generosity in her life. She had rice, *shona moonger* daal, different types of fries, fish-head soaked in gourd, fish curry, curds, sweets and, of course, paan or betel leaf. Trina was extremely hungry and started gorging on the food as if nobody was watching.

When her plate was almost empty, Trina remembered that Prabhat wasn't around.

'Oh, I should wait for him,' she said softly.

The ladies started giggling at her innocent comment. Trina had food smeared on her face but stopped abruptly. Her new friend Parama convinced her that it was okay for her

A New Chapter in Trina's Life

to eat. They laughed and teased Trina as she quietly finished her food, blushing.

At around five in the evening, Prabhat returned with a carriage full of goods and necessary items. Trina looked on in awe as Prabhat entered her room with two labourers. They filled the room with an almirah, bed and bedding, a musical instrument, new cutlery, crockery, betel leaves, fresh fruits, drinks and more. Prabhat mounted paintings on the wall. He handed over new clothes to Trina along with an expensive pair of gold bangles.

Trina couldn't believe her eyes. *What have I done to deserve so much love and care!* she wondered. One servant was also appointed, who would be at Trina's service round the clock.

Trina felt like a queen with all the love and riches that Prabhat was showering on her. But the moment she remembered her poor parents back in the village, she felt upset. However, the sadness didn't last long, for she was easily distracted by the new riches in her life.

Prabhat reassured her, 'Just be happy and relax. If you need anything at any time, let me know and I will get it for you. If I am not there, talk to the landlady. And, for your day-to-day needs, the servant will attend to you at all times.'

Trina felt like she was dreaming and didn't want this dream to end. She hugged Prabhat tightly and thanked him for saving her.

༄

What happened later that evening came as a rude shock to Trina and turned her life upside down.

The house that had looked so peaceful and quaint in the morning, despite the presence of so many people, turned into a busy marketplace in the evening. Trina couldn't comprehend what was happening. The house and its residents underwent an incredible transformation. Every room and the main courtyard were lit up with hundreds of lamps and decorative diyas, or hand-made mud-pot lamps. The choicest of hand-fans were displayed all over the house. The servants stood outside the rooms of the women holding large fans.

The womenfolk turned into beautiful brides in the evening. They decked up in riches, draped gorgeous saris and flaunted their jewellery. Their kohl-painted eyes coupled with sparkling bindis on their foreheads made them look even more attractive than they had seemed in the morning. Trina thought they were competing to look better than one another. She observed that the women who didn't have gold jewellery covered themselves in brass and copper jewellery. The bejewelled women looked like what Trina had always dreamed of looking as a bride, and she couldn't stop ogling at them.

As the evening progressed, these gorgeous women emerged from their rooms and stood in the balcony, facing the streets. Some of them stood provocatively at their windows, most of their upper body almost protruding out. They were smiling, laughing and even winking at the men passing by. Trina was bemused to witness this course of events.

Soon, the house which had looked like an 'all women's abode' changed its character completely. Men started entering the house, some alone and some accompanied by more men. They looked smart and wealthy, and sported expensive clothes. Some even wore jewellery. As they entered, the women flocked to them and welcomed them into their rooms. Some men were familiar to the women while others appeared new.

The attendants followed the women and started making the guests comfortable with hand-pulled fans. Trina stood by her window and witnessed everything. She could see men in every room apart from hers. The women were cuddling up to them, some were singing and dancing. In some rooms, liquor was being served along with food. In other rooms, there was sound of chatter and laughter. The men had generously spread attar on their attire and the scent was intoxicating. Trina also noticed Prabhat gayly talking to a few men and accepting money from them. He counted the money and then directed the men to Parama's room.

The celebrations continued till late in the night. Trina felt uncomfortable when she saw some women sitting on the laps of men. A few couples were kissing and getting physically intimate. In a few rooms, the candles were blown out and attendants were asked to leave. The woman in those rooms closed the doors with their men or man inside the room. Even though it was dark, through the light emanating from an adjacent room, Trina could see the interior of Sabita's room.

The man in Sabita's room was undressing her. He seemed to be in a hurry. Trina couldn't see Sabita's face but she could sense that Sabita had consented to the act. The man showered money on Sabita and she greedily collected the notes. Then, Trina saw the naked bodies of Sabita and the man wrapped around each other, rolling over the bed. She was so aghast that she turned away from the window.

Trina couldn't relate to the obscenity that she saw her new friend indulging in. A fear started clouding Trina's mind. Scared, she shut the door and didn't leave her room that night.

As the night grew deeper, Trina mustered up courage to peep through her window again. She noticed Parama's room, where the candles were still glowing. There were two men in that room. One was holding Parama by the hair and the other was busy experimenting with the lower part of her body. All of them were naked. The men laid her down on the floor. Trina's heart was pounding out of her chest and she was sweating heavily; she turned around and closed her windows. What was this place? What was she doing here? These questions kept clouding her mind till she fell asleep, exhausted.

Trina woke up the next morning to a vigorous banging on the door. She leapt to her feet and opened the door. It was Prabhat. Trina hugged him instantly, and began crying. Prabhat sat down with Trina and started stroking her hair gently. He didn't ask her anything.

Trina felt like a sinner who had left her family and village behind and eloped with a stranger. But then, Tara had introduced her to Prabhat and initiated her into love. So, Prabhat was not really a stranger. He had also left his family for her. But why did he do that? Trina knew that she was not married to Prabhat and so, if he left one day, she wouldn't be able to stop him. What would she do then? She wouldn't be able to return to her parents, as she had already become an outcaste...a fallen woman. Trina couldn't get rid of the conflicting thoughts that cluttered her mind.

Prabhat kept sitting by her side quietly, patting her head and comforting her.

Life in Sonagachi

Trina couldn't come to terms with the fact that she was living in a brothel. Once Prabhat left for work, she packed her things and prepared to leave.

As she was about to step over the threshold, she heard Rashmoni Debi call out to her.

'Ma Trinoyoni, where are you going so early in the morning?'

Trina's throat turned dry. 'I-I just want to step out and look around. I have never been to such a big city.'

A gatekeeper blocked her way as Rashmoni walked towards Trina in a hurry. Trina was terrified as the tall, muscular man moved closer to her.

Rashmoni signalled the gatekeeper to stop.

Then, she politely asked Trina, 'What do you want to see? Let Prabhat babu come back, he will show you around Calcutta.'

'But, I...I want to go out,' Trina insisted, shaking in fear.

'You can go out if you want. But, before that, let me tell you what might greet you outside!' Rashmoni Debi said in a stern voice.

Trina stared at her, scared and confused.

'You are in a *beshya polli* and, right now, this house is the safest place for you. You will stay here like a princess, indulge in luxury and enjoy life. But once you step out, the world will rip you apart. Vultures are always on the lookout for easy prey like you. You might be kidnapped and smuggled to some dungeon and be forced to please a hundred sexually starved beasts. And if, by chance, you are ear-marked for the British Army, God help you! Forget about a good pay, you will not even get an hour free to yourself.

A woman walking alone on the streets will raise more eyebrows than you can imagine. But, more importantly, you will not be able to get out of this maze called Sonagachi. So, I would advise you to quietly stay home and befriend the girls. If you want to explore the city, let Prabhat babu show you around once he's back.'

Rashmoni Debi started walking back towards her room, not waiting for Trina's response.

Tears welled up in Trina's eyes. Suddenly, she felt a tap on her shoulder.

Trina turned around and found Parama smiling. 'Come with me, sister.'

Trina held Parama's hand and walked back to her room. They sat down on a mat inside Trina's room and Parama fetched her some water. Trina sipped lightly and sniffled.

Parama calmly explained while stroking Trina's hair, 'Rashmoni Debi is like a mother to us. She will never force you into anything. You are very beautiful. Don't waste your youth. Cry as much as you want today. But remember that, to survive, you need money. You will make lots of money and live like a queen if you stay here. But if you leave, nobody will be able to protect you.'

Now that Parama and Rashmoni Debi had both said it, there was no way Trina could avoid or think that she was in a different place. She asked in a heavy voice that was shaking with fear, 'Can't I go home to my parents?'

Parama replied, 'You have dishonoured them by eloping. You are a Kulin Brahmin widow. Do you think anyone will accept you back in your village? Even if they do, why do you want to spend your life following the strict rituals of widowhood?

Besides, I heard that there is a big problem with *neel chaash* in the villages. My procurer Bishnu babu told me. The sahibs have brutally beaten up my father because he refused to bow down to their demands. I don't even know if he will live.'

'Did you try going back to your parents?' Trina asked, disconcerted.

'What is the point? They cannot accept me. Like you, I, too, was a new widow when I fled.'

Trina's mind drifted back to her small village and to her favourite Tara didi. Life had been challenging in Burdwan, but it had still been innocent and acceptable for Trina. She still thought that it was an accident that she had ended up in Sonagachi.

Suddenly, she said, 'Had Tara didi been alive, I never would have ended up here!'

'Who was she?' Parama asked curiously.

'She was a pious Vaishnavite woman who introduced me to Prabhat babu. She always watched over me and took care of me and my family when we had no money. Unfortunately, she died due to a terminal disease.'

Parama looked at Trina and teared up slightly as she stroked her friend's cheek. 'Oh, my dear Trinoyoni! You are so naïve! You didn't even realize that she was a procuress. She sold you to Prabhat babu!'

Trina was speechless and refused to believe Parama, even though her words were slowly starting to make sense, and things that had remained hidden from Trina were now becoming clear. 'No...no...that's not possible! She gave all her life's belongings to my parents. She...she took care of my every little need...'

'Why would a poor Vaishnavite lady go out of her way to help you? You were her source of income. I also came to this brothel in the same way. An uncle in my village introduced me to my pimp. We fell in love and fled,' Parama countered, although she remained calm and kept trying to placate the newcomer. She understood how much of a shock and change Trina was going through.

Trina was too overwhelmed to speak coherently. She wondered if Tara had really betrayed her trust. Trina recalled how she had ignored her brother's warnings and defended Tara. She had never actually seen Tara begging but, somehow, Tara had always had money. Trina also remembered the bangle-seller episode and the kanthi-badal story that Tara had so lovingly narrated.

Parama clarified it for Trina, 'Your Tara didi must have had male friends who provided for her. But once she was past her youth, perhaps the men were not interested in her anymore. That's when she found you and sold you to Prabhat babu. Else, how would she make money? Sadly, this is how most of us have reached this brothel.'

'Sold me? But Prabhat babu is not into this dirty business,' Trina retorted.

Parama took a deep breath and said, 'Prabhat babu is a procurer. He buys young girls from villages through his contacts, like your Tara didi.'

'You think Tara didi donated everything to my parents on her deathbed as atonement for her sins?' Trina asked, aghast.

'Yes, my dear sister,' Parama said and hugged Trina.

As she reminisced about her days with Tara, Trina couldn't hold back her tears. The days when the two would just go to fairs and visit temples felt so far away. All the times that Tara had lovingly oiled and massaged Trina's hair before bed and all the jokes they had shared. Had it all been a ploy to abduct Trina and throw her into slavery? Had Tara always seen Trina as a fallen woman? Trina tried wiping away her tears, but they wouldn't stop, as she realized more and more what a dangerous and evil world she was in. Could she trust anyone?

'Why did this happen to me? Why I am so unlucky?' Trina cried.

'No, my sister, you are not,' comforted Parama. 'Would you be able to see this big city if you were living the life of a widow in your impoverished village? You would have to follow those agonizing rituals that Brahmin widows have to. Your life would have been a living hell. True, your Tara didi made money by selling you. But she opened up a whole new world for you—one where you have the right to choose. Nobody will punish you or beat you up for eating meat or laughing loudly. If your babu is happy, you have nothing to worry about. And...' Parama paused and looked at Trina mischievously.

'And what?' Trina asked, rubbing her eyes.

Trying to cheer her friend up, Parama added with a smile, 'And it's obvious that Prabhat babu loves you.'

Parama's words instantly brought a smile to Trina's lips.

The Transformation

Over the next few days, Trina underwent a remarkable transformation. Aided by her friends, Parama and Sabita, she came to accept her surroundings and started feeling some ease about living in Sonagachi. She closely observed the women of the house and gradually started to enjoy their company. New men entered their rooms each night and the women tried their best to entertain them. Most of the men kept coming back and always asked for the same women. Sometimes, they brought other richer men with them. The women were delighted to entertain these wealthy men who always paid them generously and gifted them expensive jewellery.

While the young women got busy with their babus, Trina noticed the older women sitting by their windows in provocative clothing, singing seductive songs to lure new customers.

Trina's relationship with Rashmoni Debi was cordial. After a few initial hiccups, mostly due to Trina's reluctance to stay in Sonagachi, she discovered that Rashmoni Debi was not as strict or hard-hearted as her gait suggested. Instead, like Tara, Trina found a capable teacher and matriarch in

Rashmoni Debi. Under her guidance and the support of the other women in the house, Trina's training to perfect the art of pleasing men began. She gradually started growing comfortable talking about sensual matters and got rid of the taboos she had internalized early in her life. She mastered the trick of using the right expressions to convey an erotic desire. She also started taking singing lessons from Rashmoni Debi, who was a brilliant singer and patron of Hindustani classical music. Trina excelled at vocals and enchanted everyone with her soulful singing. She wasn't miserable anymore. Though she missed her parents and often thought about how her life would have been had she not been knee-deep in sin, she had no intention of returning to her village.

She enjoyed smoking, as it gave her a new high. On Rashmoni Debi's insistence, Trina tried drinking too. But when Rashmoni sensed that alcohol made her uncomfortable, she advised Trina not to drink but to pose with a glass while entertaining men to give them the impression that she enjoyed drinking with them.

When Rashmoni was convinced that Trina was ready, she invited rich businessmen, babus, zamindars and traders to her house one evening. Trina was dressed in a beautiful red sari and decked in gold jewellery. She wore make-up and sensually chewed a betel leaf, as instructed by Rashmoni.

Rashmoni took great pride in introducing 'Trinoyoni Debi' to her esteemed clients.

The guests at Rashmoni's house couldn't take their eyes off Trina. They offered money to Rashmoni upfront for an exclusive evening with Trina. But Rashmoni was not in a hurry. She wanted the word to spread so that more men visited the brothel. To top it all, Trina entranced everyone with her singing.

That day, the little girl had a big realization. She was no longer Trina—the carefree girl from the tiny village in Burdwan. She was now Trinoyoni Debi—the newest courtesan in Sonagachi, Calcutta.

'You were too good,' remarked Prabhat after the guests had left. 'You will earn a lot of money. Here, keep this,' Prabhat said and handed over some money to Trinoyoni.

'You keep it, Prabhat babu. What's mine is yours,' Trinoyoni said in a husky voice. Even though she had started working, Trinoyoni was still deeply in love with Prabhat, and had silently vowed to remain loyal to him.

A few days later, Prabhat entered Trinoyoni's room with a couple of friends. Trinoyoni did her best to entertain the men. She offered them hookah, paan on a platter, sang for them, joked with them and even drank with them. Prabhat smiled at her, and Trinoyoni instantly knew that he was happy with her progress.

Though the men who visited Trinoyoni sometimes played with her hair, touched her cheeks and asked her to sit on their laps, she hadn't slept with anyone but Prabhat yet. When these other men entered her room, they were always accompanied by Prabhat. Trinoyoni entertained them with music and dance and spoke with them for hours. They were crazy about the way she spoke and showered expensive gifts on her. Trinoyoni accepted them only after getting a nod from Prabhat. She was happy to be his mistress.

Soon, the number of men visiting Trinoyoni increased considerably. She was in high demand and, sometimes, the men had to queue up and wait for her. During that waiting period, other girls in the brothel were sent to entertain the men. But the men longed for Trinoyoni's company and would occasionally rebuff the other girls sent to them, insisting that they were at the brothel only to see Trinoyoni and no one else. They paid pots of money just to catch a glimpse of her or share a drink with her. Trinoyoni was now the star attraction of the brothel and had become quite prominent in Sonagachi within a few weeks. Soon, men were desperate to see her even during the day.

Life had never been better for Trinoyoni. She had food, clothes, jewellery, ample money to pamper herself and a house where she could live without any restrictions.

However, a problem arose when one of Prabhat's friends demanded to meet Trinoyoni in his absence. She was hesitant, but the man was ready to pay three times the price for her exclusive company. Trinoyoni agreed after consulting with Rashmoni, but she was worried that Prabhat might take offence. When Trinoyoni finally met that new man, he was not alone but had a group of new clients with him. Trinoyoni mustered up the courage to meet them. She dressed provocatively and entertained the group of men all day. She chatted with them, sang, shared a smoke and even danced with them. But such was her aura and personality that nobody dared to touch her without her consent.

Trinoyoni's confidence increased after that day and she began entertaining guests on her own. The money was too good to turn down. People were willing to pay any price just to enjoy Trinoyoni's company. They started gifting her expensive jewellery in Prabhat's absence. Trinoyoni accepted everything. Prabhat assured her that he didn't have any problems as long as she didn't sleep with anyone else. Prabhat's reassurance gave Trinoyoni a sense of belonging.

Trinoyoni was proud of the fact that despite being a popular courtesan, she was physically intimate with only one man. They were madly in love with each other but aware that they could never get married. After all, Trinoyoni was a widow. Despite the introduction of the Widow Remarriage Act (1856) by the British government in India, after the relentless pursuits of Ishwar Chandra Vidyasagar, the predicament of the women and worldview of the people had not changed. Trinoyoni couldn't imagine that a widow could remarry, as that would be a bigger sin than embracing the life of a courtesan.

∽∾

A year later, Trinoyoni was devastated when Prabhat was infected with a venereal disease. After battling for his life for a month, he died in his sleep. Trinoyoni had always dreaded the day when Prabhat would leave her, but she had never thought death would be the reason!

She cried for days and refused to meet or talk to anyone. She lay broken in her room, mourning the loss of yet another person she loved.

The Rise of the Courtesan

Rashmoni Debi and her girls stood by Trinoyoni like family. They consoled her in every way possible.

Rashmoni Debi said, 'You are my daughter, Trinoyoni. This place will remain your home for as long as you want.' Trinoyoni hugged the landlady and sobbed.

A week later, Trinoyoni's close aide, Sabita, entered the room and offered her a drink.

'Gulp it down, dear sister,' Sabita insisted. 'You will feel better. Madan babu is here to see you. Should I send him in?'

Trinoyoni grabbed the cup and gulped it down instantly. She didn't need to pose with a drink anymore. In fact, for the first time in her life, Trinoyoni enjoyed the drink.

Trinoyoni looked out of the window of her room and saw the streets filled with men, some waiting outside the building where she lived. She spotted Madan babu standing patiently, his eyes sparkling in anticipation for her. While her crying had subsided in the last few days, Trinoyoni still felt grief for Prabhat and all that he was to her. But she had to move on. Her life was still here; she was still young and pining for Prabhat would amount to the same as staying in Burdwan and observing the rituals of widowhood. She remembered what both Prabhat and Tara had told her over the years, 'Once you know how, you can have anything you want.'

'Yes, send him in,' Trinoyoni confirmed.

Madan was a well-built, forty-five-year-old zamindar who used to frequent Trinoyoni's room along with Prabhat. Madan was smitten by Trinoyoni but had never got the opportunity to get physically intimate with her.

As Madan entered the room, Trinoyoni pulled him by his *panjabi* with such force that the golden buttons stitched to his garment came off and the silk kurta ripped open. Trinoyoni picked up the gold buttons and handed them to Madan, who, in turn, pulled Trinoyoni closer and slipped the buttons down her neck inside her bright-blue sari. The buttons settled between her breasts. Madan's eyes followed them there. Trinoyoni pulled Madan's hand towards her. As Madan slipped his right-hand down Trinoyoni's sari in search of the buttons, he took his time to explore her body as she moaned in delight. Finally, Madan retrieved the gold buttons and placed them in her hands.

Next, Madan and Trinoyoni undressed and dived into a pool of erotic pleasure.

From the open windows, Trinoyoni could hear the sound of *dhaak* beats and *shondhya arati*. It was Durga Ashtami, her nineteenth birthday. The year was 1859. This was the first time she had slept with someone other than Prabhat.

Madan explored her beautifully sculpted body with his hands and his mouth. Soaked in sensual pleasure, Madan pulled her hair back tightly and pressed his mouth to hers. He continued to kiss her till she was almost breathless.

The next morning, when Trinoyoni woke up, she found a

heap of money beside her mattress along with the gold buttons and a fat gold chain that Madan had been wearing. She smiled.

That night, Madan visited again and they resumed their adventurous sexual journey. Trinoyoni made more money. Since Madan was leaving Calcutta for a week, Trinoyoni was ready to welcome other men to bed. She was surprised by how easily she had managed to move on from Prabhat's death. But she reasoned that that was because she had found a way to differentiate between love and the pleasures of the flesh. No matter what happened, Trinoyoni would always love Prabhat, nobody else could take that place in her life.

That entire week, night after night, Trinoyoni slept with new men. She looked forward to her sexual encounters and grew bolder and more experimental with each new partner.

She continued entertaining men from different strata of society: the rich, the middle class and some British civil servants as well. Trinoyoni never asked the caste of the person she was sleeping with, unlike some of her other friends.

Even though Trinoyoni didn't have a filter, Rashmoni Debi did. She was careful to send only the richest of customers to Trinoyoni. Their caste didn't matter, but their cash did.

Madan was back after a week but disappointed, as he had to make an advance booking to meet Trinoyoni.

'Why this rule for me?' he asked Rashmoni Debi, angrily.

'Money speaks Madan babu,' she responded. 'Pay more and I shall remove your queue.'

More and more men started queuing up to meet and talk to Trinoyoni. But not all of them could earn the privilege of sleeping with her.

Over the next few months, Trinoyoni evolved into a

seasoned courtesan with the richest men in Calcutta dying to spend time with her. She wasn't anyone's mistress now, but always in demand. She entertained her guests with wine and meat provocative dancing.

Rashmoni Debi was overwhelmed with Trinoyoni's popularity. She sent her own maidservant to look after Trinoyoni after a hard day's work, to be her masseur and cook. Trinoyoni could afford to pay a higher rent too, which pleased Rashmoni immensely.

Sometimes, when she was alone, Trinoyoni felt guilty about the grave sin she was committing as a widowed Hindu Brahmin woman. But then she remembered what being a committed married woman had gotten her. She had had to sacrifice her jewellery and clothes for the sake of Priyogopal's dowry. A life of comfort and luxury was not hers to have if she was going to be chaste or morally upright. Trinoyoni thought about the gifts she was being showered with and all the guilt was forgotten.

After Prabhat's death, life became easier than Trinoyoni had imagined. She grew independent and accumulated an enormous amount of wealth through her many admirers.

In a couple of years, Trinoyoni's name and fame spread far and wide. She became extremely choosy about the men she met and entertained. From serving them drinks to chatting with them, offering hookah and betel leaves in beautifully decorated silver cutlery, Trinoyoni excelled at everything. She also learnt to talk on diverse subjects, like politics and culture.

One zamindar asked her thoughts on politics, and Trinoyoni confidently commented, 'Politicians will come and go. But sex is immortal.'

The zamindar burst into laughter. Most admirers found her sense of humour alluring.

As her wealth multiplied, Trinoyoni became fussier about her customers. Sometimes, she turned down customers only because she was not in the mood. Trinoyoni would get anything that she demanded from her clients. Nobody turned her down. Rather, she was treated like a princess. Most of the time she would be covered in jewellery from head to toe. From gold to the most rare and exquisite gems and jewellery, Trinoyoni had everything that only the rich could afford. She had several hundred jewellery pieces, loads of cash and jars full of *mohor* stocked in her almirahs.

By 1861, Trinoyoni realized that she had a space crunch at her current residence. Looking at her increasing demand and the growth in her wealth, she decided to move to a new house in Sonagachi. Before leaving, she paid Rashmoni Debi a lumpsum amount and distributed gifts among her sisters.

⌇∞⌇

Trinoyoni's new house was a palatial double-storey house. Everyone in the area knew that it was the house of the richest courtesans in the locality, and one of the richest in Calcutta. She posted two security guards outside the house, dressed in traditional attire and the trademark pagdi. She had a total of five servants and maids to run the house and usher in her guests. The interiors of the house were impeccably done up. Her bed was gifted to her by the raja of a neighbouring princely state. Trinoyoni took pride in her horse-drawn carriage, manned by a personal driver.

Trinoyoni's wealth had made her snobbish. Her servants would screen customers before they were allowed to enter her home. Some customers even started bribing the servants to catch a glimpse of Trinoyoni. Housewives were scared that once their husbands met Trinoyoni, they would never return home. Imported scents from Persia also found a way into her house, courtesy her admirers.

After a few years of being established in Sonagachi as the greatest courtesan of Calcutta, Trinoyoni met a man she wouldn't forget for the rest of her life. His name was Rudrapratap, and he called himself a *samaj sebi*. He was not rich, but he had a magnetic charm that people found hard to resist. Trinoyoni was drawn to him the first day she had spotted him smoking outside her balcony. She asked her security guard to show him in.

'Why did you call me here?' Rudrapratap asked, rather miffed. 'I have no work in this beshya polli'.

Trinoyoni said calmly, 'Will you not talk to me because I am a beshya?'

Rudrapratap explained to Trinoyoni that there was a world outside Sonagachi and more important things than just gold and pleasures of the flesh.

'Can you read and write?' he asked.

Trinoyoni shook her head in response.

'Then you cannot comprehend the change we are trying to bring.'

For the first time in years, Trinoyoni felt very small in front of a man—one whose wealth did not come from money but from his knowledge. Rudrapratap was an active member of the Brahmo Samaj and believed in change through positive social reforms. Trinoyoni liked talking to him so much that she requested him to come back to her.

'I will pay you the money you need for your initiatives,' she said.

Rudrapratap returned the next day with some books and magazines. He read out from the books to explain to Trinoyoni how the common people were being deprived of their rights by the British government. He spoke about the changing society and the Bengal Renaissance. He told her about Brahmo reforms, and she listened to him, mesmerized.

However, this friendship was short-lived. Rudrapratap was arrested by the British police and Trinoyoni never heard from him again. Even after being released from prison, Rudrapratap never tried meeting Trinoyoni again, which sent her spiralling into a depression. She gradually got out of it by constantly reminding herself that people and clients will come and go but her wealth will remain. She took refuge in her possessions and money.

Ram Babu

Ram Chandra Dutta was a young, good-looking man from a very poor family. His wife and parents lived in a village in the Nadia district of Bengal and Ram worked in Calcutta. Although he began his career as a real estate broker, he was easily distracted and often resorted to gambling to cover his losses. Always on the lookout for money-making opportunities, Ram found himself in the world of brothels and soon became a broker.

He had heard about Trinoyoni Debi and knew that it was futile to go to her house unless he had a super-rich customer with him. One day, he met a wealthy zamindar from East Bengal who was visiting Calcutta to explore the beshya polli at Sonagachi. Ram saw this as the perfect opportunity to play the middleman and strike a deal between the zamindar and Trinoyoni. He befriended the zamindar and praised Trinoyoni so much that the man was mesmerized and couldn't wait to meet her.

Dressed in a dhoti-kurta, with the zamindar in tow, Ram reached Trinoyoni's palatial bungalow. He requested the zamindar to wait outside in his horse-drawn carriage and walked up to the house. After inquiring from Trinoyoni's gatekeeper, he learnt that she was unwell and not interested in meeting clients. Ram was worried that if he failed to introduce the zamindar to Trinoyoni, he would have to return the fat advance payment that he had accepted, parts of which he had already spent to pay off debts. He tried his best to convince Trinoyoni's attendants that the richest guy from East Bengal was waiting to meet her.

When Trinoyoni heard that the pimp accompanying the zamindar had promised to pay her any amount of money she desired, she realized that it would be foolish to refuse this prospect. She ordered her attendant to escort the young zamindar inside the house.

As the zamindar waited for Trinoyoni, the servants began waving fans at him to make him comfortable. Not spending too much time on dressing up, Trinoyoni stepped on to the balcony facing the inner courtyard of the house.

Ram could barely hold his excitement after the zamindar paid him the remaining money. As he began to leave, Trinoyoni spotted him from the balcony and couldn't take her eyes off Ram, who kept staring at her in silent admiration. Trinoyoni was instantly attracted by the simplicity in Ram's demeanour and the childish cheer on his face.

I have never seen such a beautiful woman in my life! Why did I wait so long to meet her? Ram wondered in awe.

Trinoyoni was dressed in a bright yellow-green banarasi sari with detailed zardozi work. She was wearing the finest gold jewellery. Deep black kohl defined her eyes, and her shiny hair was neatly tied into an exquisite bun. Her bindi, made of kumkum and outlined with a dash of sandal, added to the calmness of her excessively beautiful face. Her delicate hands were covered with gold bangles. The sound of her anklets as she walked down the stairs added to her exquisite beauty.

Trinoyoni finally looked away from Ram and set her eyes on the zamindar, who was staring at her with his mouth wide open.

'Ahem...excuse me, zamindar babu,' Trinoyoni said in her soft, firm voice.

The mesmerized man managed to close his mouth and mumble, 'Yes, Trinoyoni Debi!'

Stealing a glance at Ram, Trinoyoni said, 'I would request your friend to have lunch at my house.'

'Oh...that's not required. He is not my friend. He is just a middleman of no social standing,' the zamindar scoffed.

'Any person who enters my house is my atithi and as you know, guest is God. I cannot let the poor soul leave my house without having a meal, at this hour no less. That will be a great sin and I am sure you wouldn't like me to be such a monster, would you?' Trinoyoni said coyly, fluttering her eyelashes at the zamindar.

The zamindar, who couldn't take his eyes off Trinoyoni, replied, 'Ah...yes, of course. Ram babu, have your lunch before you leave.'

Ram couldn't find his voice. Somehow, he managed to lower his head and nod. Then he folded his hands and thanked Trinoyoni with a smile.

'Ah, what a divine name,' thought Trinoyoni. She repeated 'Ram, Ram, Ram' in her mind and felt her heart pounding faster.

'Now, can we proceed, Debi?' the zamindar asked, greedily.

'Yes, please come with me,' Trinoyoni instructed, unmindfully.

The zamindar followed Trinoyoni to a large, beautifully decorated bedroom. Two servants greeted the zamindar with fresh fruit juice and sweets served on a silver plate. Soon, paan and hookah were also served. The zamindar was looking for a solitary moment with Trinoyoni but she said lovingly, 'Let me have the honour of serving you lunch.'

'As long as you feed me with your own beautiful hands,' he replied with a wicked smile.

Trinoyoni burst into laughter, which was music to the zamindar's ears.

While entertaining her wealthy customer, Trinoyoni's eyes began searching for Ram. She had ordered her servants to ensure that he ate well. After chatting with the zamindar for some time and letting him touch her cheeks and neck, Trinoyoni made an excuse to go out to the balcony to catch a glimpse of Ram before he left. From her second-floor balcony, Trinoyoni could clearly see Ram walking towards the main gate and hoped that he would look for her. Just before he exited, Ram turned around and looked up towards the balcony. Trinoyoni flashed her infectious smile and Ram had no doubt that they would meet again soon.

Trinoyoni returned to her room, where the rich client was waiting with two gold coins in his hand. Trinoyoni's eyes lit up when she saw them. As she invited the zamindar to her bed, thoughts about Ram consumed her completely.

When Ram visited Trinoyoni the next day, the servants didn't ask any questions. Trinoyoni sat in front of him and offered him hookah. Neither of them uttered a word for a long time.

Finally, Ram said, 'Trinoyoni Debi, I do not have the money or the social standing to afford your company. I apologize for wasting your time. I must take your leave now.'

As he stood up with folded hands, Trinoyoni said, 'Wait, Ram babu. I know you don't have money. If money was all I needed, my servants would not have allowed you into my house.'

Over the next few weeks, Trinoyoni and her Ram babu became intimate as they poured their hearts out to each other. They started seeing each other more often and Ram began introducing Trinoyoni to rich clients, which helped his brokerage business stay afloat.

Trinoyoni and Ram's bond grew stronger and they soon became passionate lovers. Ram had no qualms about Trinoyoni getting physically intimate with others as that fetched them an enormous amount of money.

In 1862, twenty-two-year-old Trinoyoni was at the peak of her career. However, she also became more finicky about her customers. While, initially, Trinoyoni had been open to sleeping with any man who had enough money, she now refused to meet anyone who wasn't a wealthy Hindu Brahmin. She would meet a Kshatriya man only if he was a prince or had royal lineage.

Trinoyoni started dressing in a more dignified manner

too. Earlier, her dressing would provocatively expose her slender neck, her thin, sexy waist and her long, fair arms, sporting gold bangles and broad gold arm bands. But now, her sari was draped in such a way that it covered almost her entire body, including the full length of her arms, the nape of her neck, as well as her waist. Besides, she wore so much jewellery that her hands were not visible anymore, just her palms and fingers.

Earlier, when a rich customer visited, she would bend down on the pretext of tying her payal, inviting the rich man to caress her neck and take a sneak peek at her cleavage. Men were so swayed by her perfect contours that they couldn't wait to slip cash and jewellery inside her sari.

After a few years of success, however, Trinoyoni became arrogant and overconfident about her abilities as an enchantress. She reasoned that since she was the greatest courtesan of Calcutta and men from all over Bengal came to see her, she should protect the wares people were paying for more closely. While earlier she had attracted customers by showing her skin and bosom, she now did the same by covering herself up, which intrigued the men who had already heard of her fame.

One evening, a few months after they had fallen in love, Ram returned from work earlier than his usual time and knocked on Trinoyoni's room. She was with a client and asked him to wait till she was done entertaining him. Ram patiently waited and as soon as the client left, he entered Trinoyoni's room. She ran towards him and flaunted the gold bangles her new customer had gifted her.

Ram looked at her with deep pain in his eyes.

'What's the matter?' Trinoyoni asked, keeping the bangles aside.

'I don't want you to sleep with anyone else anymore,' he stated.

'But why?' she asked softly, trying to hide her happiness.

Ram took a deep breath and said, 'I cannot share you with anyone. It breaks my heart and makes me furious when I imagine you with someone else. I might just kill myself,' he said, in angst.

Ram had assumed that, like Trinoyoni, he would be able to separate the feeling of love they had for each other from Trinoyoni's profession. But after the first few weeks, every time he saw a client enter her house, he was filled with rage and jealousy. Trinoyoni's love was not enough for Ram anymore. He wanted to have all of her. He wanted to possess the most desirable woman in Bengal.

Tears welled up in Trinoyoni's eyes and she hugged him. 'I must die before you utter such horrid words again. I shall do as you wish,' she promised, knowing well that she wouldn't be able to keep her word.

That day onwards, Ram would walk inside Trinoyoni's room at any time he desired, even while she was entertaining a client. Trinoyoni loved him too much to ask him to leave, even when she sensed that the client was uncomfortable in Ram's presence. Trinoyoni planned and arranged to meet with her clients only when Ram was out of Calcutta.

∞

For several years, Trinoyoni successfully managed to hide

her love affair with Ram from her customers, scared that it would affect business and dry up her regular income. Ram's futile attempts at reviving his brokerage business didn't work, and he failed to make any profits from either his business or from his gambling. By the time Trinoyoni turned twenty-eight, Ram was bankrupt.

Heartbroken at his financial misery, Trinoyoni requested Ram to move in with her. She knew that it was a risky proposition because, if prospective clients saw that a man was living with her, they would think twice before paying up to meet her. Part of Trinoyoni's allure in Sonagachi was that no single man could entirely have her; which is why rich patrons threw mountains of money and jewellery to make it possible, even if for a few hours. If they saw that she was living with a man, Trinoyoni would lose all prospects of earning any money off her body. Yet, she decided to live with Ram in the same house.

'Ram babu, we cannot get married. But we can stay together like a couple in my humble home. Of course, if you wish to stay with your wife and family in your village, I will pray for your happiness. But, if you are in Calcutta, I will be honoured if you live with me.'

'I wouldn't be able to marry you even if you were not a prostitute,' Ram replied. 'You are a Kulin Brahmin and I belong to a much lower caste. Nowadays, I have noticed that you do not accept customers who are not Brahmins. Why do you want to stay with me then?'

Trinoyoni was silent for a while. She took a deep breath and said, 'When I am with you, I don't think about money. I have never seen God, but I am sure he looks like you.'

Ram moved in to Trinoyoni's house soon after.

Manik

Trinoyoni's life was full of bliss. While she was not drawing clients like she did when she had started, there were enough brought to her house through her reputation, which allowed her to afford her expenses and live comfortably in her house. Moreover, she had found love in Ram's arms, something she had never thought she would after Prabhat had passed away.

What was missing from Trinoyoni's life, and what she knew she could never have was domestic happiness. She knew that being a courtesan and living in Sonagachi had enabled her to own and receive things and gifts, but it had come at the cost of not being married or living in a harmonious home. That life had been lost to her the moment her husband Priyogopal had married her. She had Ram, but they had to be covert about it all so as to maintain the veneer of Trinoyoni being available to her clients.

Moreover, Trinoyoni could never be a mother. She could not afford to be pregnant, which would take her out of the market for over nine months, and then there were the bodily complications of childbirth, which would destroy her career. Even though she pined for the joy of holding a baby and raising the little one herself, Trinoyoni knew that Sonagachi was not a place for a child to grow up in. It wasn't a place that allowed mothers to live peacefully either. There were times when Trinoyoni would see a mother swaddling her baby while she was out in the city. The sight would break her heart and she would be unable to do anything for the rest of the day.

One day, after her customers had left, Ram said, 'I have to tell you something.'

Trinoyoni's heart skipped a beat and she thought Ram was going to leave her. She looked at him intently, trying to prepare herself for the heartbreak.

'I...I have a son. He must be a year old now. I have never seen him,' Ram said, tears trickling down the corner of his eyes.

Trinoyoni was more than relieved. She was surprised at the sudden revelation, and the mention of a child kindled hopes in her that she had learnt to kill repeatedly.

'What is his name?' she asked, gently.

'Manik.'

Trinoyoni closed her eyes and imagined a tiny toddler crawling towards her. She felt an instant connect with this baby she had never met.

'What does he look like?' she asked in her excitement.

Ram didn't respond and Trinoyoni repeated her question.

'Like I said, I have never seen him,' Ram managed to reply in a guilt-ridden voice.

With a heavy heart, Trinoyoni said, 'Oh. Then you must visit him. You are lucky to be blessed with a son.' She regretted the statement the moment she uttered it, for it reminded Trinoyoni of her inadequacy. She feared that once he saw his son, Ram would abandon her and she would be left all alone.

Ram sighed, 'Yes, I wish to see him too. I am worried about him. My family back in Nadia is neck-deep in debt and misery; they can barely afford to feed him, let alone paying for his education.' He looked worried.

Trinoyoni instantly got up from the bed, still thinking about Manik and his needs, 'Oh, you must send them money every month. I have so much money. It is your money too, Ram babu. Please use the money and save your family.'

Ram changed the topic, as he felt uneasy talking about his financial problems, 'Let me read out another story to you tonight.'

Trinoyoni understood that he didn't want to talk about his son anymore. So, she quietly listened to him as he lovingly read out stories from the books that he had bought for her.

The next morning, Ram said, 'I am very happy with you. But I feel miserable that you are supporting me. As the man, I should earn and provide for my mistress.' The thought had been gnawing at him for quite some time, but after Trinoyoni declared that she wanted to financially support Ram and his destitute family, it made him feel small, even though Trinoyoni had said everything out of love.

The word 'mistress' hit Trinoyoni hard but then she knew that was the truth. An idea struck her, one that would not change things significantly, but would alter them slightly so that Ram would feel like he was contributing and not just being a leech.

Trinoyoni suggested, 'Why don't you become my manager then? Filter my clients and look after my guests. I am anyway tired of managing money. There's so much that

I don't know where to keep it! It will be good if you start managing my finances.'

As she spoke, Trinoyoni handed over her almirah keys to Ram, who willingly accepted her suggestion, vowing to manage her finances and make her richer.

Soon, Ram was managing Trinoyoni's finances, taking care of her daily needs, and buying groceries and other essentials for the house. Whenever Trinoyoni needed money, she would ask Ram, who would open her locker and hand over the cash to her. She blindly trusted him and Ram didn't have the heart to cheat her. He always looked for ways to increase her income and sometimes asked Trinoyoni to curtail her expenditure. He also spent money to indulge in his own *babugiri*, which helped him network and fetch new clients for Trinoyoni.

Ram was the man of the house now and Trinoyoni was happy to lead her life according to his wishes. She gave Ram full control over her life and respected him as the husband she never had.

Despite Ram's efforts and plans at saving money, by 1872, Trinoyoni's finances were beginning to dry up. At thirty-two, she was still remarkably beautiful and charming, but her strict manners were starting to put-off her clients. Moreover, rich clients who came from far-off places to spend exclusive time with Trinoyoni now had to bear Ram's company too. They couldn't get a moment alone with Trinoyoni because Ram was always around her like a bodyguard. The clients felt cheated and often asked for a refund. Once they found out that Trinoyoni was Ram's mistress, their interest in her waned, as Trinoyoni had feared would happen. The same people who would queue up for the 'debi darshan', didn't consider pursuing Trinoyoni worth the effort now. She had ceased to be an erotic goddess.

Soon, the number of people visiting Trinoyoni started decreasing. She would make every effort to dress up and entertain her guests. But people would leave her house earlier than usual when they realized they wouldn't get any physical intimacy from Trinoyoni and had to contend with the presence of Ram around her. Trinoyoni started losing her regular customers one by one. Suddenly, there were no new customers anymore.

One day, being denied her exclusive company, a client commented angrily, 'If you stick to this man all the time, why do you even expect us to come? You are old now, Trinoyoni Debi. There are many young options available in the market. We come here to talk to you, not to your broker. I am never coming back here. Such a waste of time! You just spoilt my mood, you whore!'

Soon, other clients got abusive too. Trinoyoni tried to strike a balance between her personal life and the clients but failed. Ram had become extremely possessive of her and didn't want to see her entertaining anyone. He would get livid if he ever found Trinoyoni alone with another man.

Trinoyoni didn't want to lose Ram at any cost. She was deeply in love with him and could not bear the thought of being without him. So, when, one by one, the babus left, she didn't try to stop them. She also realized that she was past her prime and no match to the young girls in the market flaunting their beautiful bodies.

Trinoyoni's main concern was her economic situation.

The same customers who used to spend a fortune on Trinoyoni now refused to spare even a penny for her. Gone were the days when people would adorn her with jewellery. Trinoyoni desperately tried to hold on to her savings now. Unfortunately, she had no option but to start meeting her expenses from her savings. Paying the gatekeepers and five servants, maintaining the horse-drawn carriage and the huge house—everything was becoming difficult. Ram also had several miscellaneous expenses: babugiri, spending on theatre, travelling in a horse-drawn carriage, etc. that had to be met and were a drain on Trinoyoni's resources. Trinoyoni realized that without a steady income, she would become bankrupt very soon and return to the state she was in during her childhood in Burdwan. Besides, if they wanted their current business to continue, Trinoyoni and Ram had to maintain their lavish lifestyle. People looked at Trinoyoni as a wealthy courtesan and she didn't want that image to change. Appearances were important to snag new clients. However, with each passing day, it was becoming increasingly difficult to make ends meet. Trinoyoni had no option but to ask the servants and security guards to leave.

A few days later, Ram received a letter stating that his wife was on her death bed. She had been suffering from terminal cancer for some time and wanted to see Ram one last time. Ram hadn't visited his wife even once in the past four years, when he had left home to come to Calcutta while she was pregnant.

Even when Ram received the letter, he was reluctant to travel to his ancestral home to meet his wife and son. Though upset and fearful of losing him, Trinoyoni understood that it was Ram's duty to visit his ailing wife and to take care of Manik, who she still thought of fondly since Ram had mentioned him three years ago. She spent hours convincing him to visit his family. Finally, when he agreed, Trinoyoni forced him to take money from her savings. Her heart sank as he left. She was certain that he would never return to Calcutta. The fear paralysed her, and, for almost three entire days, Trinoyoni did not stir from her room.

However, Trinoyoni was pleasantly surprised when Ram returned within a week, his 4-year-old son Manik tagging along. Trinoyoni learnt that Ram's wife had died as soon as he had reached the village. After completing her last rites, Ram had sold off his house and the little piece of land he owned. He knew he had to return to Calcutta, as he couldn't imagine a life without Trinoyoni. So, he had packed whatever little savings he had along with his wife's jewellery and moved back.

'This will help us survive for a few days at least,' he told her.

But Trinoyoni was not paying any attention to Ram now. Her eyes were fixed on little Manik, who was running around the house with starry eyes! Manik was a beautiful child with deep eyes and dimpled cheeks. Trinoyoni picked him up and planted a kiss on his cheek.

'He is my son from today—my Manik.' The young lad stared blankly at Trinoyoni as she held him.

Over the next few days, Trinoyoni became obsessed with Manik and tended to all his needs like a mother. She fed him, made his bed beside her, played with him and listened to his songs and stories for hours together. Manik sang very well and Trinoyoni was mesmerized. Ram was relieved to see the closeness between Trinoyoni and his son.

Over the next six months, Trinoyoni focussed on being a doting mother and stopped entertaining clients altogether. She was about to exhaust her savings. She started mortgaging some of her jewellery to run the house. At any other time, Trinoyoni would have thought of letting go of her jewellery as the worst thing that could happen to her. She had held on to the pain of having to let go of her jewellery to pay Priyogopal's dowry. But things were different now. Ever since Manik had entered her life, Trinoyoni had stopped paying attention to any material comforts or luxuries. Manik had given Trinoyoni a purpose in life she did not know she had, and the child was her crown jewel now. She could do anything for him.

Though she had let go of her servants, she held on to her favourite horse-drawn carriage for a long time. She somehow managed to feed the horses and pay the charioteer's salary. But when the time to sell the chariot came, Trinoyoni, while feeling sad about getting rid of her prized possession, calmed her heart by reminding herself that it was all for Manik.

Meanwhile, Ram struggled, in vain, to revive his old brokerage business. He had been out of touch for over a decade and it was tough to re-establish himself. To survive, Ram resorted to gambling and petty theft. He needed investment and Trinoyoni's jewellery saved the day. He would go out to play cards with a group of wealthy people and trick them into emptying all their money on the table. Then, he would either mix sleeping pills in their drinks and flee with the money or win by cheating them. He had learnt to change his appearance and for each gamble, he began disguising differently.

Trinoyoni helped him with the planning and gathered the sedatives secretly. She requested one of her old customers to get the drug in lieu of a sexual favour without Ram's knowledge.

Meanwhile, the rise in criminal activities in Calcutta and its adjoining areas had reached an alarming level. Matters came to a head when an Anglo-Indian woman was brutally murdered in the heart of the city. After much introspection, the British Indian police decided to add a new wing to the police department, primarily to investigate criminal cases. Accordingly, the detective department was set up in Calcutta in 1868. The detectives who joined this team were addressed as darogas. A daroga was trained to be insightful and cultivate an eye for detail. The British hired Indian detectives for this job because they knew that Indians would be able to interpret the mindset of Indian criminals better than their British counterparts. Several highly efficient Bengali darogas started operating in Calcutta with the intention of nabbing criminals on the prowl.

Soon, Ram realized that it was getting increasingly difficult to manage his life of crime alone; he needed help. One evening, he broached the subject with Trinoyoni.

'If we want to improve our financial condition, we have to make some serious plans. These gambling and stealing acts cannot continue for long. The risk is high and the gain is peanuts.'

Trinoyoni nodded. 'What do you have in mind?'

'Many ideas are cooking inside my head. The problem is, I will not be able to execute such ideas alone. I need a partner,' Ram said, wearing a worried look.

'I will help you. Tell me, how can I be of use?' Trinoyoni offered.

'Are you sure, Trinoyoni? There is no stepping back once we start walking this path,' Ram warned.

'You know me well. I will never go back on my word.' Trinoyoni had a strong sense of right and wrong, and while she would have preferred to earn her money honestly, the truth was, in this world, honest people do not earn much. She knew this, having entertained the richest and the vilest men in all of Bengal for years. She reasoned that stealing from the rich would not be a sin. She reminded herself again that she was doing this for her son. Her Manik.

The Dangerous Duo's First Victim

In the mid-1870s, the Bengal Presidency witnessed a terrible famine characterized by a severe scarcity of food and an unprecedented growth in deadly diseases. People in the rural areas died of starvation and several villagers moved to the city in search of food and sustenance. This filled Calcutta up to the brim with unemployed and destitute people, which led to a tenfold increase in crime. The police could not do much in the face of the desperation of people and, as a result, most criminal cases went unsolved and unreported.

In nineteenth-century Bengal, young boys from rich families were prohibited from indulging in vices, like smoking and drinking. If anyone was caught in the act, the family's reputation was tarnished. So, young adults would explore these vices in secret hideouts, along with like-minded friends. Ram was on the prowl to befriend such individuals since it would be easy to dupe them. There was also the added advantage of escaping severe repercussions if caught since the boys and their families would want to keep the misfortune hidden or risk having their reputation tarnished.

Ram's first victim was a seventeen-year-old boy named Madhob Kumar, the son of a wealthy businessman from

North Calcutta. One afternoon, he spotted Madhob smoking nonchalantly outside an old factory. He looked around to make sure that there was no one who would recognize him and then slowly approached the young thrill-seeker.

'Young man, may I have a word with you?' Ram asked.

Startled, Madhob hid the cigar and nervously asked, 'Who are you?' He started looking around in paranoia, afraid that he had been caught.

Ram realized that he needed to defuse the situation. He stepped back and assumed an air of casualness, 'Don't be so alarmed. I just noticed you smoke the same thing as I do. It's rare to find someone smoking this stuff.' Ram feigned being impressed with Madhob's choice of cigar.

'Oh, this? It isn't available in Calcutta. A friend got it from London,' Madhob relaxed a little once he realized that it wasn't a person looking to lecture him on morals or rat him out. He smiled when he sensed an adult appreciating his choice.

Ram tried to continue the conversation, taking out an expensive-looking cigar himself and lighting it, 'Ah, I see! But it is not difficult to procure. I enjoy it whenever I want. When I party at home with my friends, I enjoy it along with drinks.' He let out a puff of smoke in Madhob's direction.

Madhob nodded and started walking towards the factory. Ram quickened his pace to catch up with him, trying to appear agreeable and friendly.

'I don't want anything from you. Please let me go,' Madhob said as he noticed Ram beside him. The boy had started sweating now, once again believing that something was wrong. He quickened his pace.

'But what happened, young man? I know it's not allowed in your house, but are you afraid to smoke?' Ram asked. In response to Madhob's pace, he decreased his own, trying his best to not scare the mark. While his face looked at ease, Ram desperately wanted this ploy to work. They had just sold off the chariot a few days ago and were already in need of more money.

'I-I am not afraid of anything. Please leave,' Madhob insisted, but slowed down once he saw that Ram was not following him.

'Okay! I am leaving. I thought you are a courageous young man who enjoys his smoke. Since I live in the next lane, I wanted to invite you over for a smoke. But I understand, you are not interested. I shall take your leave,' Ram concluded. Then, he turned around and slowly started walking towards his house, making a point to flamboyantly wave around his cigar and blow smoke rings as he did so.

'Wait! One minute!' Madhob squealed almost instantly. 'What if my family gets to know?'

'How will anyone know?' Ram said with a smirk on his face. He knew Madhob had taken the bait.

The boy shrugged his shoulders. Then, still suspicious of the adult, he blurted, 'But you don't even know me! Why would you invite me to your house?'

Ram finished his cigar with a flourish and said, 'I am Ram Chandra Dutta and I run a brokerage business. I have many friends who enjoy a smoke. But I realize you are too young to appreciate a good cigar. It's alright. Some other time perhaps.' He slowly turned around to leave.

Madhob looked confused. He was very interested in

smoking with this man, since the way he had lit his cigar had been with the air of a connoisseur, and the young boy wanted to have that same confidence and enjoyment that Ram showed. But he was wary as well. 'I can come, but is it okay if I get my friends too? They also enjoy good cheroots. We will pay for the cheroots we buy from you.'

Ram turned to face Madhob and flashed him a smile, 'You and your friends are most welcome! Don't worry about paying me. I just like having nice company and people who appreciate a good smoke. I have a good collection; you'll like it, I am sure. See you tomorrow then!' Ram responded. Madhob nodded enthusiastically. 'Yes, we will be there in the evening. Thank you!'

Trinoyoni and Ram made elaborate plans to welcome their new guests. The house was beautifully lit. Servants and gatekeepers were hired for the day. Trinoyoni cooked her speciality *mangsho bhaat* and other delicacies. Ram made elaborate arrangements for drinks, hookah, betel leaves and cigars.

At around 7.00 p.m., four young men arrived at Trinoyoni's house. Ram received Madhob and his friends gleefully. He escorted them upstairs to the big room, where a cellar had been set up. Most of the drinks on display were fancy bottles with minimal alcohol in them. Ram had mixed water with the drinks so that the cellar looked well-stocked. The young boys, aged between seventeen and nineteen, were excited by the display.

When Trinoyoni entered the room, dressed in her best, the boys couldn't stop ogling at her. She looked stunning. She served them food lovingly and chatted in her honey-coated voice. The boys looked at her in awe as Ram served them drinks.

Then, Trinoyoni began singing in her mellifluous voice, mesmerizing everyone. The boys realized that she was a courtesan and were even more intrigued now. As Trinoyoni entertained the guests, Ram collected their glasses for a refill. The boys were bowled over by Trinoyoni's magnetic charm. They started measuring the contours of her body with their lustful gazes. They had never interacted with a woman at such close quarters. Trinoyoni allowed the anchal of her sari to accidentally drop off her shoulders a few times, allowing the boys a closer look at her curves. Ram could sense that the boys wanted to get closer to Trinoyoni.

As he handed them their drinks, one of Madhob's friends remarked, 'How do you manage to smoke so many cigars, Ram babu?'

Ram laughed. 'There is nothing quite as good as the taste of an exquisite cigar, don't you think, young man?'

'You have an amazing collection of imported drinks Ram babu...you have the best of everything...' Madhob declared in a slurry voice and took another big sip of his drink that had been prepared by Ram.

'Yes...s...s...' the others added in an inebriated chorus.

Ram and Trinoyoni kept communicating with their eyes while the boys got drunk. Ram quickly finished another cigar. Trinoyoni gestured with her hand to reassure Ram that the dose was strong enough for their guests and he need not smoke so quickly!

But Ram didn't want to take any risks. He collected the ashes from his cigar carefully and kept them ready to be mixed with the next drink. The deadly concoction of cigar-ash and alcohol created the desired intoxicating affect, but the boys had no way of understanding that.

Even before they could finish their third drink, three of the guests, including Madhob, had passed out. The fourth person had started on his next drink but before he could bring the glass to his lips, he, too, collapsed.

Trinoyoni and Ram quickly sprung to action. They searched the boys thoroughly and robbed them of their valuable personal belongings. They collected a great deal of cash, some watches, expensive perfume, silk handkerchiefs, gold chains and gold rings.

By late evening, Trinoyoni and Ram had dragged the unconscious boys out of their house in the darkness. After ensuring that nobody had seen them, Ram and the hired gatekeeper dragged the boys further till they reached the end of the lane. After dumping the boys, as soon as they were about to walk back to Trinoyoni's house, Madhob coughed.

Worried that Madhob would regain consciousness, Ram pushed Madhob further towards the edge of the lane. The young boy's head hit a stone and he started bleeding profusely. Seeing the amount of blood loss, the gatekeeper and Ram fled the scene. Once back home, the gatekeeper extracted more money from Ram because he was sure that Madhob was dead.

The next morning, the inebriated boys woke up at the police station. They were embarrassed about what had transpired the previous night and didn't report anything to the police. They were not even aware that Madhob had died. The police dismissed Madhob's death as an accident. When the friends conversed among themselves, they couldn't remember how or when they had left Ram babu's house.

A few days later, based on a complaint lodged by Madhob's influential father, the police started questioning people but failed to gather any leads. They questioned Ram, too, and he feigned ignorance about the whole episode. When the police interrogated Madhob's friends, they remained tight-lipped about their secret evening at Ram babu's house. They were scared of anyone finding out they had been robbed by a courtesan and her procurer, knowing it would bring dishonour to their families. Though devastated by Madhob's death, the friends chose to delete this horrifying episode from their lives.

Trinoyoni advised Ram to lie low for a few days because the police were still investigating Madhob's death.

After a month, Ram set out to find his next victims. He befriended them, attended gambling parties with them and lured them into visiting his house. Trinoyoni and Ram followed the same pattern that they had started while entertaining Madhob and his friends. Trinoyoni served drinks and cigars to the guests, along with meat and sweets. Ram spiked their drinks with cigar ash, following which they became unconscious. Trinoyoni and Ram robbed them of their belongings and threw them out of the house. However, they were careful not to physically harm anyone. When the men woke up at the police station, they kept quiet to avoid a scandal and turning into the laughing stock of the town.

However, once, a young man complained to the police about Ram and Trinoyoni, claiming they had robbed him after intoxicating him. But when the police questioned the duo, Trinoyoni confidently said that when the man left her house in an inebriated state, he had all his belongings with him. Trinoyoni spoke so smoothly that the police were completely convinced.

Though the police were convinced, this young man spread the news in his circles about a middle-aged beshya and her helper who cheat vulnerable young men. The news spread like wildfire and, suddenly, Trinoyoni became a villain who was not just a courtesan but also a fraudster. Rumours about Trinoyoni's character spread like the plague. She had to cover her face to go to the market. People who recognized her openly hurled verbal abuses at her and some shopkeepers refused to conduct business with her.

One day, a group of angry women pelted pebbles at her while she was returning from the market. One of the pebbles hit her forehead and she started bleeding. Trinoyoni ran home crying.

Ram decided that it was time to stop this dangerous cheating game. This abrupt end to a lucrative scheme worsened their financial situation. The jewellery Trinoyoni had mortgaged had to be sold off because nobody was willing to lend them any money. Trinoyoni had already gotten used to the jewellery not being hers since it had been mortgaged for several months, but finally selling it off injured her as much as the stone that the women had thrown at her.

But she had more important things to worry about. Manik was growing up fast and worries about not being able to care for him properly consumed Trinoyoni. She couldn't let her son suffer. This was when she started plotting another criminal adventure, with her partner-in-crime Ram ready and willing to help her.

Crimes Surrounding Marriage

The year was 1875. One evening, Ram returned home with Narayan Mallick, an old associate from his brokerage days. Trinoyoni welcomed him and served hookah and sweets.

While smoking his hookah, Ram asked, 'Narayan babu, are you sure you will be able to arrange this? Will they trust you?'

Narayan confidently replied, 'Don't worry, Ram babu. I am not fixing the match myself. The matchmaker is the groom's uncle. Though he lives in Calcutta now, he keeps travelling to his village and has now taken the responsibility of finding a bride for his nephew.'

Ram asked, 'But the groom's family is respectable. Why didn't they find a bride in the village? Should we be aware of any ailment that the family is hiding?'

Narayan laughed. 'No, Ram babu! The groom is completely healthy. The problem is that these people are pure Srotriya Brahmins. This class of people is strictly barred from marrying anyone apart from a *shudhha* Srotriya. Now tell me, if they don't find a Srotriya bride, how will they take their family name forward?'

Ram replied after some thought, 'That is an excellent proposition.'

Narayan continued, 'The other problem is that though the groom's late father was respected, the family is poor. Rich families want their daughters to get married in wealthy families, even if it is as the tenth wife. Besides, the rituals of Srotriyas are much different than those followed by other Brahmins.'

Trinoyoni interrupted. 'Yes, in this community, the groom's family has to pay *kanya pon* to the bride's family before marriage.'

Narayan nodded. 'The amount can be anything—from a penny to thousands of rupees. Add to that the jewellery, bridal trousseau, bedding, etc. The groom's family also pays for the dinner served to the guests at the wedding.'

'But, how will these poor people arrange for the money?' asked Ram.

'Exactly!' said Narayan babu. 'Due to a lack of funds, they are unable to find a suitable bride in the village. The forty-year-old groom lives with his widowed mother in a tiny hut. They have a piece of land that they are ready to sell if they find a Srotriya bride for their son.'

'Will they agree to our offer?' asked Ram.

'Yes, because they know that our prospective bride belongs to a Kulin family, even though she is not very young,' said Narayan.

Ram anxiously asked, 'Narayan babu, have you explained everything we discussed yesterday to the groom's uncle?'

Narayan replied, 'Oh yes! The groom's uncle is aware that the girl is the only daughter of a pure Srotriya. After her father's death, she and her mother moved to Calcutta to live with her maternal uncle's family. I have explained that neither the mother nor the uncle has any money as a result of which the girl is still unmarried at fourteen. All they need is a Srotriya groom, regardless of their financial condition.'

'How much can they spend?' Ram asked impatiently.

'I asked for five hundred rupees for wedding preparations, buying jewellery, etc. They agreed because they assumed that the jewellery would remain with the bride. I also asked for an extra hundred rupees to organize food for the guests. They agreed immediately because I didn't demand any konya pon.'

'Let's invite them at the earliest,' Ram stated.

'They want to meet the girl next week and get over with the wedding. Have you arranged for the bride?' asked Narayan, deeply concerned.

Trinoyoni promptly replied, 'The girl is a beauty. I will deck her up when the Srotriya family comes to see her. You don't have to worry a bit.'

'Please tell me something about the girl,' Narayan asked curiously.

Trinoyoni smiled and guided the men to her balcony. Pointing to the line of slum-rooms adjacent to her house, Trinoyoni said, 'Priyadarshini resides in one of those rooms. She is fifty years old now. She was sold off at this beshya polli at the age of ten. Soon, this hell became her home. She used up all her money in her youth and now she is almost penniless. Her struggle for survival breaks my heart. One day, she bought a one-year-old girl from another courtesan, paying peanuts for her. She brought up the little girl like her own daughter and named her Chhaya, who is not illiterate like me or Priyadarshini. She is beautiful and clever and knows how to read. She has agreed to play the role of our Srotriya bride. But we will have to share half of our earnings with Priyadarshini.'

The men agreed.

Narayan said, 'Before anything else, we must rent a house in a decent, residential area. The groom's family cannot know that she resides in Sonagachi.'

'But where is the money to rent a house?' Trinoyoni asked.

Ram added, 'Nobody will rent out their place for a day. We need to rent it for a month, at least.'

Trinoyoni decided to break her piggy bank, which she had reserved for emergency funds. The next day, Ram rented an old, double-room house in a *bhadralok* neighbourhood.

The landlord said, 'The house is lying empty because the last tenant died by suicide. So, if you don't want to stay here, I understand.'

Ram calmly replied, 'I don't have any issues with that. We will perform a puja and yajna before entering the house to ward off all evil.'

To impress the landlord, Ram projected himself as a god-fearing man who was in Calcutta on an official visit and needed temporary accommodation.

The landlord said, 'Don't mind me saying this but I have never seen you around nor have you come here on any gentleman's reference. I am a little sceptical about renting my house to you because so many crimes are being committed around the city these days.'

Ram decided to handle the situation tactfully. He grimly said, 'I apologize for not being able to come here earlier. My wife was unwell and my little son wasn't letting me leave the house. I can pay you the rent in advance if you wish. However, if you are uncomfortable trusting me, then I must take your leave.'

The landlord responded, 'I am sorry, I didn't know you had a family. You are welcome to rent the house. And yes, I would like the advance payment please.'

Ram collected the keys and left after paying the full month's rent to the landlord.

Later that evening, Trinoyoni, Ram and little Manik shifted to the rented house along with Priyadarshini and her daughter, Chhaya. They settled in separate rooms, with their bare minimum luggage. Trinoyoni and Priyadarshini cleaned the house overnight. They didn't beautify the house much because the groom's family knew that Chhaya's family was very poor.

A few days later, escorted by Narayan, the groom and his family visited Trinoyoni's rented house. Trinoyoni greeted them with folded hands and a lowered head. She kept her head and face covered with her saree, just the way women in respected families were expected to do. She also kept quiet because it was not ladylike for women to speak unless they were spoken to.

Trinoyoni had another valid reason to hide her face. She had been a popular courtesan in her younger days because of the stories surrounding her beauty and wealth. As a result, she was worried that someone in the groom's family might recognize her because her clients used to be wealthy upper-caste gentlemen.

After exchanging a few pleasantries, the groom's family requested to see the bride.

Trinoyoni had trained Chhaya to act like a coy, demure bride and not show her face till asked. Chhaya walked into the room slowly, holding Trinoyoni's hand. She wore a simple, bright-red cotton sari and had her face covered with her anchal. She sat down beside her pretend uncle, Ram babu, who introduced her as his niece.

'Can we see her face please?' requested a relative.

Trinoyoni slowly lifted the anchal from Chhaya's face. The groom's family was highly pleased to meet Chhaya. They asked her several questions and the groom couldn't stop staring at her. She appeared shy, kept her head lowered, and answered each question slowly and softly like an obedient girl. The eldest uncle from the groom's side blessed the girl with a mohor, confirming the match.

Chhaya was asked to return to her room. Her heart was beating fast, as she had never lied in such a manner before.

The eldest uncle said, 'There is a good date for the wedding seven days from now.'

Ram acted a bit hesitant and responded, 'It's a very short time to organize a marriage.'

'We can pay you some money to organize things quickly. Will that help?' the uncle asked.

Ram folded his hands and said, 'As you wish.'

The next day, Ram sold off the gold coin they had received from the groom's uncle to a broker and divided the money between him, Trinoyoni, Narayan and Priyadarshini.

The Fake Wedding

'What if they find out that I am a prostitute? What if someone from the groom's family recognizes me? I have entertained many customers, didi, and I am really nervous now. What will happen to me if they find out?' Chhaya was nervous the day before the wedding. She felt breathless and her voice petered out.

Trinoyoni brushed her hair and replied calmly, 'You are an intelligent girl, Chhaya. Just remember that this marriage is going to make you very rich. You will have your face covered most of the time and nobody will recognize you. Just stop worrying.' She attempted to pacify Chhaya the same way Tara had done years ago, when the little Trina had tried to drown herself in the river.

In between gasping for breath, Chhaya hugged Trinoyoni and started crying.

'Be strong, my dear. Everything will be fine...trust me,' Trinoyoni assured her and tried to calm Chhaya down. The weeping gradually subsided, once Chhaya was sufficiently convinced about the plan. Trinoyoni and Priyadarshini had spent a considerable amount of time planning the wedding so that it went off without a hitch and none of them got caught. The plan, as far as Trinoyoni and Ram knew, could not possibly fail.

As Chhaya walked back to her room, an unexpected guest appeared at Trinoyoni's doorstep.

Ram was rather surprised to see the middle-aged man, who introduced himself as the groom's eldest cousin. As Ram welcomed him into the house, the cousin handed him fifty rupees to organize the *gaaye holud*. Delighted to receive this bonus amount, Ram tried his best to hide his excitement. He requested the cousin to take a seat and offered him sweets and water. Pleased with Ram's hospitality, the cousin sat down and chatted with Ram while enjoying the sweets.

As he was about to leave, the cousin noticed a bunch of cigars on the window sill of the living room. Appalled, he smarmily commented, 'You don't have money for your niece's wedding but you can afford imported cheroot?'

Ram was alarmed at the discovery. He thought on his feet and pretended to laugh heartily, 'Hahaha! I can't even dream of touching such expensive cigar. How dare I smoke it? My landlord is a chain smoker. He was here last evening and must have left it by mistake. I'm sure he will be back any moment to reclaim his cheroots,' Ram lied.

The relative seemed to buy the excuse. 'Oh, I see! I'm sorry for accusing you in such a way. The truth is, I have had a fascination for cheroot but never had the money to afford a smoke,' he said, staring at the cigars.

Ram grabbed the opportunity and asked, 'Why don't you try one? My landlord smokes so much, he won't even notice.'

The groom's cousin greedily picked up three cigars and left, thanking Ram for the gift.

The Fake Wedding

Trinoyoni and Priyadarshini decorated the house beautifully on the day of the wedding. Guests started pouring in. Narayan invited many of his acquaintances to pose as relatives of the bride. Trinoyoni invited some of her prostitute friends from the brothel in Sonagachi where she used to live. She was careful to invite only middle-aged women who were no longer active in the business.

The groom arrived at the rented house in a horse-drawn carriage. Dressed in a white dhoti, white cotton shawl and *topor*, he was welcomed with the traditional *borondaala* by the women of the bride's family. He wore sandalwood make-up on his forehead, just like the bride.

The fake purohit performing the marriage rituals was such a brilliant actor that even Ram was surprised. He impressed everyone by speaking highly of the bride's family and her Srotriya caste. The groom's family, who had emptied their life's savings to make this marriage possible, had no inkling that the bride was a non-Srotriya prostitute.

However, while the wedding rites were in progress, a few relatives from the groom's side expressed concern about the relatives from the bride's family. Several of them were worried that there were too many women at the function who were unaccompanied by men. They were also rather surprised that there were no children from the bride's side at the function.

The groom whispered to his best friend, 'Brother, are all women in Calcutta so shameless? I have never seen women interacting with men so openly!'

The groom's maternal aunt asked her husband, 'Do women from respectable families behave like this?' She was referring to Trinoyoni's friends from the brothel who were talking loudly and laughing among themselves, and seemed to have no sense of restraint.

The aunt shared her concern with the others and an elderly person approached the priest, 'I am worried, *purohit thakur*. Everyone says different things about the bride. It seems that nobody knows her or her family well. I don't get a good feeling about this marriage. You know how fraudsters have spread in this city! Since you are a Brahmin, I want to seek your advice if this is a good family. Do you think it is wise to proceed with this marriage? Are we being cheated?'

The priest calmly replied, 'You have nothing to worry about! The person who has mediated this marriage is highly respected. You are insulting him by doubting his judgment. The bride may be poor, but the family is cultured and respected.' Though not completely convinced, the elderly man nodded and walked away.

Ram and Narayan ensured that all the pending money was collected from the groom's family before the completion of the marriage ceremony.

Chhaya looked gorgeous in her bright-red cheli sari and jewellery. As she sat on the *biyer piri*, her face covered with betel leaves, she shed tears silently, asking the Lord to forgive her for this grave sin, and praying that she wouldn't get caught.

Dinner was served after the marriage ceremony. The guests appreciated the food, all of which had been cooked by Trinoyoni and Priyadarshini, and forgot about their apprehensions regarding the marriage once their appetite had been satisfied. Most of the guests left after dinner, apart from the groom's friends and siblings, who stayed back for the bashor raat celebrations.

The following day, after the completion of some more post-wedding rituals, it was time for the bride's send-off. As the newly married couple got ready to leave, Priyadarshini and Ram also joined them. Trinoyoni vacated the rented house soon after the guests left because, in case the plan failed, they didn't want the police to be able to track them down. Trinoyoni packed all her belongings and, along with Manik, shifted back to her own house in Sonagachi. Narayan also decided to go underground for a few days. Everyone waited eagerly to hear from Ram babu.

It had been over a week and Trinoyoni still hadn't heard from Ram. Worried, she decided to contact Narayan babu. As she got ready to leave the house, she saw a horse-drawn carriage stop in front of her house. Trinoyoni rushed to the balcony anxiously and said a silent prayer as she saw Ram babu, Chhaya and Priyadarshini getting off the carriage.

Once the trio were inside the house, Priyadarshini helped Chhaya remove all her gold jewellery. Soon, Narayan walked in with a jewellery broker. The broker closely examined the ornaments and offered two hundred rupees.

'But this is worth at least four hundred,' protested Narayan.

'This is stolen jewellery. If you can sell it anywhere at a

higher price, do that.' The broker retorted. He knew, by the looks of it, that these people were involved in some kind of fraud. It was clear to everyone in the room that the broker was the one in power here. He was about to leave but Ram stopped him.

He said, 'Let's settle at three hundred. You know this is all pure gold.'

'Two-fifty. And that's final,' the Marwari broker replied firmly.

Narayan and Ram, seeing that they could not negotiate anymore, agreed to the amount, which was still significant. They reminded the broker to keep the transaction a secret.

As soon as the broker left, Ram divided the money among his partners-in-crime.

After everyone departed, Trinoyoni asked Ram, 'How did you escape? I am dying to know! I hope nobody suspected you?' After a week apart, the two hugged and couldn't let go, continuing the conversation while in each other's arms.

'Forget all that. See what I got for you,' Ram lovingly tied a gold chain around Trinoyoni's neck. He knew how much she missed having jewellery and wanted to keep something that didn't need to be sold. 'Wow! This is beautiful,' Trinoyoni squealed in delight. 'Now, tell me what happened when you were there!'

Ram untangled himself from Trinoyoni's hug. All of a sudden, he looked tired. He sighed and sat down on the diwan, 'You know what I feel bad about, Trinoyoni?' started Ram. 'The groom's family is really decent. They took very good care of us during our stay at the village. For a while, we had forgotten that the marriage was fake. I started treating Chhaya like my niece and Priyadarshini as my own sister. The *bou-bhat* ceremony was spectacular and everyone blessed Chhaya. I feel horrible that I corrupted the dharma of so many Brahmins who unknowingly ate food served by a prostitute. What a grave sin I have committed!' He looked up and smacked his forehead repeatedly as he cried.

'Please don't blame yourself, Ram babu,' pleaded Trinoyoni as she tried to stop him. 'We all planned this together.'

Ram sighed again, 'Everything was going well till the groom's uncle asked if we wanted to take the newly-weds back to Calcutta for the *Ashtamangala* ceremony. That was our golden opportunity to escape.'

Trinoyoni gasped. 'Oh...and then?'

Ram cleared his nose and shifted on the diwan, 'We started from the village, took the train and reached the station together. On the way, I was thinking about how to get rid of the decent man but I couldn't. He was so enamoured by Chhaya that he wouldn't let her out of his sight even for a moment. Chhaya also fell in love, I think. Anyway, I had to end it somehow.

We got off the train and I requested that jamai babu get some tea for us. The poor man immediately approached a nearby tea vendor. I had given him some money. As soon as he turned around, we rushed towards a horse-drawn carriage and fled. We didn't even look back once. Chhaya couldn't stop crying.'

Trinoyoni's eyes were moist.

'God will never forgive me,' said Ram. 'I cheated a

Brahmin family.' The two cried together at what they had done. Trinoyoni recalled how Tara had cheated her Brahmin parents and sold her off to her procurer and first love, Prabhat. She realized, with some horror, that she was slowly turning into the same person.

∽∞∽

A few days later, during an evening when Ram and Trinoyoni were plotting their next scheme, a series of loud knocks on the main door alarmed them. In a panic, Trinoyoni rushed to her first-floor balcony and spotted a group of muscular men at her door.

'Ram babu, I don't have a good feeling. Some scary-looking men have surrounded our house,' she informed Ram, who hurried downstairs and opened the door. The men barged in and one of them gripped Ram's neck. Though scared, Ram tried to maintain a brave front.

'What is the matter, gentlemen?' Ram asked as he tried to free himself from the hands around his neck.

'Don't pretend as if you are seeing us for the first time, Ram babu. I will drag you to the police station and report the crimes you have committed,' lashed out one man, as the others behind him raised their voices and agreed with the accusations.

Ram yanked the man's hands away from his neck and declared sternly, 'Leave my house right now or I shall call the police. The daroga of the local police station is my friend.'

The men looked at each other, but, before leaving, made sure to let Ram know that they knew about his crimes, 'You better watch out, Ram babu. Your days are numbered'.

'You know the daroga?' Trinoyoni asked as she fetched Ram a glass of water. He was panting and clutching his throat with one hand and took the glass of water in the other.

'Of course not. I had to get rid of these goons. Don't worry. They will never come back.'

Even though he didn't believe he had said it, Ram was right. The men never returned. However, people in the locality started talking about Ram and Trinoyoni. There were rumours that Ram had duped an innocent Brahmin man. Together with the incident surrounding Madhob's death a couple of years ago, rumours around the two started swirling about with twice the intensity they had the last time.

However, back in Chhaya's fake husband's village, everyone kept their mouths shut. They couldn't take the risk of sharing this fraudulent experience with their relatives. If the news spread, the Brahmin community would disown them. Thus, the family made up a story about the bride's death. No police complaint was lodged against Ram.

༺༻

Over the next three years, Ram and Trinoyoni cheated seven more Srotriya men and their families by showcasing Chhaya as the pretty, impoverished and demure bride. They made good money and managed to stay away from the police. However, as Chhaya grew older, it became increasingly difficult to find a suitable groom for her fake marriage. Slowly, Ram and Trinoyoni realized that Chhaya was no longer useful to them.

Trinoyoni tapped her sources at Sonagachi but nobody could supply her with young girls. More importantly, her brothel friends didn't want to be a party to her risky criminal adventures. When all endeavours failed, Trinoyoni and Ram had to stop their fake-wedding business. As they started plotting their next crime, Priyadarshini tried to convince Chhaya to resume entertaining customers again. Though reluctant, Chhaya obliged since the money was too lucrative to turn down.

One evening, Priyadarshini came crying. 'I am devastated, sister Trinoyoni. Help me.'

'What has happened?' Trinoyoni asked, worried.

'They have taken my Chhaya away, those men from the British army!' she howled.

'What? When?' Trinoyoni asked.

Priyadarshini couldn't respond. She collapsed to the floor, unconscious.

∞

Later that night, Ram applauded Trinoyoni on her brilliant idea of selling Chhaya to the British soldiers as a sex slave. He gave her a thick bunch of notes to count—the money he had received after selling Chhaya.

Trinoyoni began counting the money hurriedly and Ram lit an imported cheroot...both more interested in the risk-free profit they had made. The horrors of turning into Tara long forgotten, Trinoyoni could only think of the things she would buy for Manik with the money and, perhaps, if there was some left over, she could buy some jewellery too.

The Infamous Kidnappings

One day, while returning from a jewellery broker's shop, Trinoyoni noticed a little girl standing near her house, crying. She looked lost.

Trinoyoni walked up to her and asked, 'Are you looking for someone, my child?'

The girl, who looked barely six or seven years old, kept crying.

'Where are your parents? Do you stay nearby?' she asked, gently. But the girl didn't utter a word.

'You must be hungry. Come home with me and eat something,' Trinoyoni suggested. At the mention of food, the girl finally looked at Trinoyoni, who lifted her up and carried her inside the house. She served the girl some freshly-made sweetened cheese curd, known as *chhena*. The little one ate hungrily, as if she had been starving for days. After drinking some water, she looked at Trinoyoni with kind eyes.

'I want my mother,' she said.

'What is your name, my dear? Trinoyoni asked.

'Mohor,' she softly said.

'You stay here, Mohor. I will look for your mother,' Trinoyoni assured the girl, gently stroking her hair. Once the girl fell asleep, Trinoyoni stepped out of her house and surveyed the locality. It was a scorching summer afternoon and the roads were completely deserted. After looking around for a while, Trinoyoni stepped back inside her house.

By evening, Manik and the little girl had become friends. Trinoyoni felt happy seeing the kids laughing and playing around the house. She was often worried about Manik not having friends in the locality. The scene before her made her smile.

When Ram returned home later that evening, Trinoyoni told him about the girl. Ram listened attentively and said, 'You have just given me a brilliant business idea!'

'What?' Trinoyoni asked, excited.

'I overheard a few people at the tea stall today. They were saying that cases of missing children are rising in Calcutta. Children are getting separated from their parents in crowded places. Though the police are able to reunite some of these missing children with their parents, a large number of kids are never found. And guess why?'

'Why?' Trinoyoni asked, curiously.

'Because most of these missing cases go unreported. As you know, most families have at least a dozen children at home. So, by the time the elders realize that one or two kids are missing, it's already too late! And if these children belong to poor families, the parents don't even bother to file a missing complaint with the police!' Ram explained, his mind already creating all kinds of wicked designs for this opportunity that had landed in their laps.

'Oh, but what happens to those children?' asked Trinoyoni.

'Well, they get kidnapped, sold or are forced to beg. Sometimes, they die of starvation. The rich kids usually wear expensive jewellery. So, I am sure kidnappers target them.'

'So, our next target is such children?' Trinoyoni was slightly aghast at what she was planning to do. While Chhaya had been close to adulthood, this girl was barely able to do anything by herself.

Ram laughed and replied, 'Since you've already taken the first step, why delay?'

When Ram saw the little girl sleeping, he was delighted. 'We have to act fast. She will fetch us a handsome price. Let me contact Narayan babu immediately.'

Once Narayan joined them, the trio sat together to seal the fate of that little girl.

Narayan floated an idea to Trinoyoni, 'I suggest you groom her for three months at least. I will arrange for advance money from a brothel. She will fetch a better price if she has basic training in music and dance.'

Over the next three months, Trinoyoni trained Mohor to sing and dance well. Along with Mohor, she trained ten other girls, who Ram and Narayan kidnapped from different parts of the city. They only abducted girls because they weren't sure if boys would get them any money. Ram and Narayan found that it was pretty easy to kidnap a child wandering alone on the streets. All they had to do was lure the kids with good food. Once the kids met Trinoyoni, they didn't want to leave her. She fed them, bathed them, gave them clean clothes, brushed their hair and told them stories of beautiful princesses. Those poor girls had never received so much warmth and care in their life and were mesmerized.

Trinoyoni sometimes saw a glimpse of her childhood in them and shed a silent tear. But the next moment, she was back in business, without an iota of guilt. Trinoyoni's transformation into Tara was now complete.

Soon, Ram and Narayan began selling the girls to various brothels in Sonagachi. Seven had been sold and three were still remaining. When these three girls asked about their missing friends, Trinoyoni would lie that they had been reunited with their parents.

The risks involved in transferring the girls were increasing by the day. Most of the girls were very young and would scream when brokers snatched them away from Trinoyoni. At times, Trinoyoni found it hard to control her emotions too. But once Ram handed her the money, she forgot everything and looked at Manik's happy face to console herself.

With the rise in kidnapping cases, the police were on high alert. Ram and Trinoyoni decided to lie low for a while. That's when Narayan suggested, 'Instead of selling these girls, we can get them married. The money will be better in such deals too.'

'How?' asked Ram. He still remembered all those times they had had to parade Chhaya as a bride, and how difficult it had been to escape without getting detected.

'We will have to travel to East Bengal with the girls. I have information about at least five poor Brahmin families who will pay dowry just to get their illiterate sons married,' said Narayan. He remembered the problems they had faced the last time too. 'The families want daughters-in-law only for childbearing. That's all! And since we won't be in Calcutta, it will be easier to give any suspicious people the slip.'

Ram pondered on the idea for some time before slapping his knee. 'Let's do it. The money seems good,' Ram said. 'Besides, we cannot keep these girls at home forever!'

Soon, Trinoyoni, Ram and Narayan set off for a small village in East Bengal posing as the parents and uncle, respectively, of the girls. They met the Brahmin families and finalized the marriage proposals. The abducted girls were very young—ten years old at the most. They considered Trinoyoni as their mother and happily tied the knot.

Once the girls were married, Trinoyoni and Ram extracted as much money as possible from the groom's families and stole the bride's jewellery. Then, they returned to Calcutta and never contacted the girls again. The kidnapped girls had no inkling that they had been cheated. They busied themselves in their new lives, as any other child-bride of the nineteenth century would. Trinoyoni did not feel too guilty about the weddings because neither was anyone being harmed, nor were the girls in a miserable place. If anything, these marriages were new beginnings for them, and they were getting to experience the joys of marriage and motherhood, which had been denied to Trinoyoni. She felt that these schemes were justified because she was rescuing the girls rather than putting them in jeopardy. With every marriage and every sale, she felt a little less guilty, till Mohor's second marriage, where she did not feel even an ounce of remorse.

People were attracted by Trinoyoni's charm. When she was in East Bengal, fixing marriages for her fake daughters, some of the groom's family members were impressed by her conduct and trusted her blindly. They even agreed to send the girls back home for the Ashtamangala ritual. Once the girls were safely back in Calcutta, Trinoyoni would steal all their jewellery and arrange a second proposal for them—and Mohor was no exception.

'But I am already married,' ten-year-old Mohor told Trinoyoni when she was asked to deck up as a bride again.

'We made a big mistake by getting you married there, Mohor. Your husband is very old and he will die soon,' Trinoyoni lied. 'He doesn't have a good character and I have heard that he has a mistress. I don't want you to stay in such a house, where your in-laws will ill-treat you and your husband will ignore you. So, I rescued you from there before they could cause you any harm. The man you are marrying now will treat you like a princess.'

Mohor loved Trinoyoni very much and blindly obeyed her. A few days later, Mohor tied the knot with another poor Brahmin man from East Bengal.

Trinoyoni, Narayan and Ram made a fortune out of Mohor's second marriage. The guy they got her married to was a forty-nine-year-old weak man, suffering from an acute venereal disease. In contrast, Mohor's first marriage had been to a decent twenty-year-old illiterate boy, who had taken an instant liking to his new wife. Trinoyoni severed all contacts with Mohor after her second marriage. It was necessary that there be no contact, lest they were caught.

In the meantime, due to an alarming rise in the number of girls missing from the city, the police were on high alert. The British government had ordered a detailed investigation into the mysterious disappearance of pre-teen girls. Detailed search operations began all over Calcutta and police detectives in plain clothes started visiting neighbourhoods and raiding houses for random searches.

Thankfully, Narayan tipped Trinoyoni and Ram off about the increased scrutiny. Even though they were making a considerable profit, Trinoyoni and Ram were forced to stop all illegal activities surrounding this business of fraudulent marriages. They decided to lie low till the police pressure decreased and things returned to normal.

A Few Weeks Later

Even though they could still afford the necessities, Trinoyoni could see their savings slowly dry up, and if they did not find an opportunity within a month, they would be forced to sell the house.

The door opened and Ram rushed in, 'We must rent a place and move immediately,'

Sensing the urgency in his voice, Trinoyoni asked, 'What's wrong?'

Ram handed her a bag full of money and said, 'Listen carefully. We are going to start a new business soon. I have figured out all the details. If things go well, our miseries will finally end. We are going to be richer than ever before. I want to operate the business from a new house. In case anything goes wrong, we can safely return to this house.'

'What business will give us such high returns?' Trinoyoni asked, perplexed.

Ram said, 'Trust me. I will disclose everything in good time.'

A week later, they locked Trinoyoni's double-storey house and moved to a shanty rented house a little distance away. Manik was not happy with the move and missed the few friends he had managed to make with a lot of difficulty. Trinoyoni assured him that he would make new friends soon, but Manik continued to sulk around the house.

As soon as he was out of sight, Ram said, 'In this business, I will need a female accomplice. Would you like to be my partner or should I look for someone else? The problem is that if we team with an outsider, we have to divide the profits again.'

Trinoyoni promptly replied, 'Of course, I will work with you, Ram babu. When do we start?'

Ram was thrilled at Trinoyoni's readiness and narrated the entire plan to her. Trinoyoni felt a chill down her spine and couldn't believe her ears, but she loved Ram more than anything in the world and decided to trust him with the plan.

The Daring Daroga

Daroga Sukumar Bandopadhyay, who had been inducted into the detective department of the British Indian police in Calcutta in the 1870s, had earned wide acclaim for his brilliant detective work. Sukumar was popular among the public as the clever daroga babu. He had a penchant for marking his targets and designing elaborate plans to nab them. Sukumar was addicted to his profession of pursuing criminals and devising innovative strategies to trap them into confessing their crimes. He saw criminal cases as puzzles that had to be solved. While he was a policeman, Sukumar was not interested in the humans who were the perpetrators, because, so far, he had found these criminals to be of simple minds. His interest, therefore, lay in solving the crime as quickly as he could. Like some of his contemporaries, Sukumar was a master of disguise and had perfected the art of changing his appearance to spy on his suspects.

In the mid-1870s, Sukumar received an interesting case in the form of a letter addressed to him. The sender was Gokul Chandra Pal, the owner of Pal Jewellers, a reputed jewellery store at the heart of Burra Bazar in North Calcutta.

Respected Daroga Mohashoy,

Trust you are doing well. I am writing this letter to seek your help in investigating a critical case of theft. As you are aware, I have a jewellery shop in Burra Bazar replete with gold and silver jewellery, expensive gems and stones, and several other luxurious jewellery items. Two days back, jewellery worth twenty thousand rupees went missing from my shop. My trusted employee, Deen Dayal Singh, entrusted with the job of delivering the jewellery to the customer, is also missing.

Few days back, a princess by the name of 'Rani ji' visited my shop along with a jewellery broker called Ram babu. It seemed that Rani ji was well acquainted with Ram babu though neither me nor anyone else in Burra Bazar area have ever seen this man. Rani ji came to our shop in a deep-red, double-horse-drawn carriage. Ram babu came in a separate, single horse-drawn carriage. Rani ji didn't enter my shop. She kept sitting inside her carriage while Ram babu collected the jewellery from my shop and showed them to her. She chose whatever she liked and asked Ram babu to get the selected pieces packed and delivered to her house. Rani ji said that she would pay cash to the delivery person at her home. She also expressed interest in buying additional jewellery items later. After she left, this Ram babu stayed back while we packed the jewellery.

Then, my veteran employee, Deen Dayal, proceeded to Rani ji's house with the jewellery accompanied by Ram babu, in his carriage. Rani ji was supposed to hand over the payment to Deen Dayal for the jewellery she purchased. However, what happened after Deen Dayal left with Ram babu is a mystery! I never received those twenty thousand rupees from Rani ji. Deen Dayal is also missing. I have looked for him everywhere but he is nowhere to be found. He is a sincere and faithful employee and I am worried that something unfortunate has happened to him.

I request your help in locating my missing employee and retrieving my lost jewellery.

Yours faithfully,

Shri Gokul Chandra Pal
Pal Jewellers

Sukumar was so intrigued after reading the letter that he decided to visit the jewellery shop immediately. He was inquisitive about this Rani ji, who had visited the market with a broker. A woman from a royal family visiting a market area unaccompanied by a man from her own family was unheard of! Was this woman really a princess? Sukumar was also curious to meet the broker and the missing employee. He presumed that the trio had hatched a plot to rob Pal babu. After all, it was a matter of twenty thousand rupees!

When Sukumar reached the jewellery shop, he found the elderly owner, Gokul Chandra Pal, leafing through his company's account books. Sukumar showed the letter to Pal babu and requested him to narrate the details of the day when Ram babu and Rani ji had visited the Pal Jewellers' showroom.

Pal babu rubbed his eyes at the memory of the tragedy that had befallen him, adjusted his spectacles and started, 'Five days back, two majestic carriages halted in front of our shop. My security guards eagerly waited outside the first carriage to welcome the esteemed guest. But nobody alighted from the coach. A middle-aged man dressed in crisp white dhoti-panjabi got off from the second carriage and entered my showroom. He introduced himself as Ram Chandra Dutta, a jewellery broker. He mentioned that a princess or 'Rani ji' from a princely state was sitting in the bigger carriage. She wished to buy jewellery and he would be helping her with the purchase. However, the woman never came to my shop. Ram babu and my employees carried all the jewellery to her carriage. She selected the ones she liked and asked Ram babu to get them packed.'

Sukumar asked, 'Was she alone inside the carriage?'

'I don't know. Nobody saw her,' replied Pal babu.

'Was the woman Bengali?'

'I have no idea, daroga babu! Ram babu said she was a non-Bengali. When I heard her voice, I thought that she was speaking in broken Hindi with a Bengali accent,' replied Pal babu.

Sukumar asked Pal babu if the horse-drawn carriages had belonged to the princess.

'Since Rani ji is not a resident of Calcutta, I assume that the carriages were rented,' answered Pal babu. 'The drivers in both vehicles wore the same uniform. I guess they were hired from the same place.'

'Would you know which place they were hired from?' asked Sukumar, curiously.

Pal babu shook his head, frowning.

'Okay, what happened next?' probed Sukumar. He seemed to have an inkling about what had actually happened. But, he needed to know the entire account in detail to be sure.

'Rani ji left after selecting the jewellery. We packed all the items and Deen Dayal left in Ram babu's carriage along with the jewellery. He was supposed to deliver the jewellery to Rani ji, collect the money and report back to the shop. But I never got my money. Worse still, Deen Dayal went missing.'

'Do you suspect that Deen Dayal stole your jewellery and ran away?'

Pal babu shook his head. 'That's impossible. Deen Dayal is my oldest employee and has been working here for over twenty-five years. He has never stolen even a penny from this shop. There are ornaments worth lakhs of rupees around him all the time! I trust him more than I trust my family members.'

Sukumar nodded, 'What about this Ram babu? Do you suspect him?'

Pal babu replied in a dejected voice, 'I haven't seen him since that day and I don't know if I should suspect him.'

Sukumar said, 'Well, unless you suspect anyone else, I would consider Deen Dayal as the culprit because he never returned!'

Pal babu lamented, 'No, daroga babu. I am worried that Deen Dayal might be in trouble. I can sense it. While I want my jewellery back, I am anxious to find him too. He is an honest man.'

The daroga mulled over the details of the case for a few minutes and then said, 'I will need a list of the missing jewellery.' Considering that Pal babu was strongly vouching for Deen Dayal, Sukumar had to revise his earlier theory and now, slowly and steadily, a new one was taking shape.

'Yes, daroga babu. I have it right here.' Pal babu handed over the list to Sukumar. The detective looked at the list and put it in his coat pocket.

'I hope you will be able to identify your ornaments once we find them?' Sukumar asked.

'Absolutely! Even with my eyes closed I can touch and identify the make of our jewellery,' Pal babu responded with confidence.

Sukumar left the jewellery shop and proceeded to the police station. He called for Saptarshi Sen, one of the most efficient police personnel in his team. They discussed the case and Sukumar instructed Saptarshi to create a preliminary report. To Sukumar's surprise, Saptarshi returned with the detailed report within a day.

'I have re-examined the facts, daroga babu. There is no doubt in my mind that Pal babu's employee, Deen Dayal, is the culprit. He ran away from Calcutta with jewellery worth twenty thousand rupees. Even magistrate sahib thinks so. After I explained the matter, he issued an arrest warrant against Deen Dayal Singh,' reported Saptarshi.

Rather impressed at the quick turnaround and somewhat irritated with himself for having discounted Deen Dayal due to Pal babu's insistence, Sukumar remarked, 'Excellent! Hand me the warrant and I shall arrest Deen Dayal right away. But how are you so sure that he is the culprit?'

Saptarshi beamed, 'I met Ram babu, the jewellery broker who was in the Pal Jewellers store to collect the jewellery. He provided all the details about Deen Dayal!' He looked proud of himself.

'Ram babu?' Sukumar asked, astonished. This was an unexpected development. 'You mean, the broker who accompanied Rani ji to Pal babu's jewellery store? Where did you find him?'

Saptarshi nodded and replied, 'One of my informers spotted him in the market and contacted me. When I reached the market, Ram babu was waiting for me. I spoke to him at length about the day of the incident. He also invited me to his double-storey house. That's why I was convinced that he wasn't lying to me.'

Sukumar said, 'So, he lives in North Calcutta? Does his family live here too?'

Saptarshi replied, 'Yes, North Calcutta, daroga babu. He didn't look like a family man, but...' he hesitated.

Sensing his discomfort, Sukumar impatiently asked, 'But what?'

'Well, Ram babu lives with a courtesan. The house is full of such women... I mean prostitutes,' Saptarshi replied rather uncomfortably.

Sukumar furrowed his eyebrows, 'A jewellery broker living in a house full of prostitutes. Interesting! What information did he give you, Saptarshi babu?' Sukumar asked cynically. He had managed to find a flaw in Saptarshi's, or rather, Ram babu's narrative. He started leaning towards his previous theory again.

Saptarshi excitedly responded, 'Ram babu said that the woman was buying the jewellery for a zamindar. Deen Dayal delivered the jewellery to her in lieu of cash.'

'Who is this zamindar now? It was a Rani ji, wasn't it?' Sukumar asked, confused. The previous story had no mention of any zamindar. Where had this zamindar come from? This story already seemed to be full of holes.

Saptarshi replied, 'Err... Ram babu isn't acquainted with the zamindar. The woman was interacting on behalf of the zamindar. He is very rich and not from Calcutta.'

'This is very strange! Where was the jewellery delivered?' Sukumar asked.

'Ram babu confirmed that the jewellery was delivered to the woman inside the zamindar's house,' Saptarshi answered, starting to see the problems in the story he was narrating.

'Did you get the name and address?' Sukumar asked.

'Like I said,' Saptarshi replied apologetically, 'Ram babu doesn't know the zamindar's name nor does he have any address.'

Sukumar was getting intrigued. 'Tell me, Saptarshi, if this woman is a "princess" or "Rani ji", why was she buying jewellery for a zamindar?'

'Oh, the woman is not any Rani ji! She is the zamindar's mistress,' Saptarshi said.

'So, the courtesan had gone to the market with Ram babu? Why did she call herself a princess then?' asked Sukumar.

Now, Saptarshi was nervous. He added, 'Yes, she and the zamindar sat inside the carriage while Ram babu got the jewels to the carriage for them to select. The zamindar didn't want to be seen in a public place, that too, with a prostitute. Thus, he asked his mistress to pose as a princess.'

'This Ram babu was showing the jewellery to the zamindar and to the woman, you mean?' Sukumar asked, impatiently.

Saptarshi nodded.

'Okay, where can we find this fake Rani ji now? We should talk to this woman!' Sukumar instructed.

'That's easy. This woman lives with Ram babu and I've met her,' Saptarshi said, with a smile. Although the smile vanished just as quickly once Saptarshi realized the direction Sukumar was taking him in.

'What?' Sukumar couldn't believe his ears. 'This zamindar's mistress, who apparently paid twenty thousand rupees to Deen Dayal Singh and also posed as a Rani ji, lives with the jewellery broker named Ram babu?'

Saptarshi gulped and said, 'Yes, daroga babu.'

'And you don't think that is strange, Saptarshi babu?' Sukumar raised an eyebrow, hoping that his capable junior would see the complete picture now.

Saptarshi replied, trying to defend his reasoning, 'But, isn't that normal? After all, she is a *prostitute*.'

Sukumar frowned and asked, 'Did you talk to this woman?'

'Yes, daroga babu. I spoke to her at Ram babu's house. Her name is Trinoyoni Debi. She went to the market with Ram babu and the zamindar. She also confirmed that she paid the full money to the jewellery shop employee named Deen Dayal Singh.'

'Did you ask her about the zamindar?'

'Yes, I did,' Saptarshi replied. 'But Trinoyoni Debi told

me that mistresses are not allowed to ask about their babu's whereabouts. They consider themselves fortunate if the babu desires to see them again.' The policeman knew that this sounded suspicious, but he was hoping that the evidence would speak otherwise.

Sukumar looked frustrated. 'How about the other women in the house?'

'They are all tenants,' said Saptarshi. 'None of the women know the zamindar because they never interfere in each other's business. Besides, zamindars, princes and even British sahibs visiting the brothel is quite common. The prostitutes couldn't remember anyone in particular!'

Sukumar asked, 'Did you get the details of the money they claim to have paid?'

Saptarshi was surprised that Sukumar was doubting his abilities. 'Of course, I did. They paid a mix of notes and coins to Deen Dayal.'

'Good!' Sukumar said, adding, 'Did you ask Ram babu for directions to the zamindar's house? Or this lady—Trinoyoni Debi? Can she take us to the zamindar's house for confirmation that the money has been paid?'

Saptarshi replied immediately, 'That will not be necessary, daroga babu. I have the details of the numbered notes.' Sukumar found his faith in his junior somewhat restored. Perhaps he had been too harsh too soon.

Before Sukumar could ask anything further, Saptarshi enthusiastically continued, 'I have also verified them with the currency office, daroga babu! Magistrate sahib has already issued a stop order against currency notes bearing those numbers. And you won't believe what else I found!'

'What?' Sukumar asked.

'Bodo sahib told me that the notes were given to him by a man named Deen Dayal Singh. He wanted to exchange the bigger denomination notes with smaller notes and coins. So, as per process, Deen Dayal had to sign on every note that he deposited at the office. That's why I am certain now that Deen Dayal is the culprit!'

Sukumar praised Saptarshi, 'Commendable indeed! I am sure that's how you attained Deen Dayal's arrest warrant too?'

Saptarshi nodded with a grin.

Sukumar asked, 'Since Trinoyoni Debi is his mistress, the zamindar must visit frequently. Let's go to Ram babu's house and check when the zamindar will be making his next visit.' He still felt like he ought to follow up on his theory. Even though Saptarshi had done really well, Sukumar still found something amiss in the entire matter. And his hunch told him to try to investigate this theft from an angle Saptarshi had not yet envisioned.

'I checked already,' Saptarshi smiled. 'But that will not be possible, as the zamindar has returned to his village. Ram babu said that he usually visits once every six months.'

'Oh, I see! How about Deen Dayal's family members? What are they saying?' Sukumar asked.

'Nobody in his family has any news, daroga babu. He didn't contact them. He just fled with all the cash!' Saptarshi commented.

Ignoring the remark, Sukumar instructed, 'Can you take me to Ram babu's house now?'

Saptarshi obliged and the two policemen proceeded towards Ram's residence.

The Daroga Meets the Fraudster Duo

Sukumar was an astute detective and he could smell crime when he saw Ram and Trinoyoni together. Sukumar had run a background check on Ram and learnt about his failed brokerage business, his acts as a pimp and the fraud cases that he had been accused of in his younger days. Sukumar knew he couldn't trust this man or his pretentious accomplice.

A few years before Sukumar had joined the detective department, his neighbour had told him about a certain Ram babu who had been accused of gambling and looting several rich, young men. Sukumar didn't know why he had a strong feeling that this was the same Ram babu, though Ram was a very common name in India.

Sukumar questioned Ram and Trinoyoni briefly about Deen Dayal and they repeated verbatim what they had told Saptarshi. He nodded, pretended to believe the two and, after apologizing for any inconvenience caused, left.

Sukumar headed straight to the currency office. He requested the chief officer there to show him the notes that Deen Dayal had signed and submitted to the office. The moment Sukumar saw the notes the entire story became crystal clear to him. He smiled at the secret he had discovered, which Saptarshi and magistrate sahib had missed. His initial hunch had been right all along.

Sukumar picked up one of the notes and examined it carefully. Deen Dayal had clearly written his name and complete address on each note. Sukumar quietly put one of the notes in his pocket and left the currency office.

'Saptarshi babu,' he said softly. 'Tomorrow morning, you and I have an important task. Come dressed like a coachman.'

Saptarshi was confused. 'You mean, like a person who drives a horse-drawn carriage?'

Sukumar nodded. 'We are going on an interesting adventure.'

The next day, dressed as coachmen, Saptarshi and Sukumar headed to a place where rented horse-carriages were available. From the description of the coachman's uniform that Pal babu and his employees at the jewellery shop had provided, Sukumar had a rough idea about which office to visit.

Once they reached the place, Sukumar, who was fluent in five languages, started conversing with a coachman in Hindi.

'My friend here,' said Sukumar, pointing at Saptarshi, 'has just lost his job. Can you help him find a new one? His wife just gave birth to a son and they desperately need money.'

Saptarshi was startled at what a good actor his boss was. He decided to play along.

'Who told you that you will get a job here?' one of the coachmen waiting near the horse stables asked him.

'I met a kind man last week, who had rented two carriages from your office almost ten days back to go to Burra Bazar. He promised my friend a job. If you can help me trace the man, I will be indebted to you,' said Sukumar.

'What's his name?' the coachman asked.

'That I don't know!' Sukumar replied, innocently.

'Then how will you meet him?' laughed the coachman.

'If I see any of the coachmen who were driving those carriages, I can track him. Can you help me find them?' Sukumar feigned helplessness and Saptarshi accordingly adopted a garb of being close to losing hope.

'Oh, but so many carriages are rented daily! It's impossible to keep track,' replied the coachman, nonchalantly.

'These carriages were different. One was a deep-red double-horse carriage rented for a princess called Rani ji. The other one was for her assistant. They went to Burra Bazar and visited Pal Jewellers. They sat inside the coach while buying the jewellery.'

Another coachman said, 'Okay, let me ask around. You wait here for some time.'

A few minutes later, the coachman returned with a coach driver named Kadir who said, 'My friend Sajid's red double carriage took a princess to Burra Bazar a few days back. But what do you want to know?'

Sukumar said with folded hands, 'If you can take me to the house of the man who rented the carriage, I will be very grateful. My poor friend can get his job back then.'

Kadir thought for a while and said, 'Okay, come along. But Rani ji was not in my coach. I never saw her. The other babu was. We just followed Sajid's carriage.'

Sukumar couldn't help but ask another question, 'When you left from the jewellery shop, was the babu in your carriage?' He wondered if he had risked his disguise for this.

Kadir replied, 'Yes. He got into my coach with an old man from the jewellery shop. I can show you the house where I dropped them. But you have to pay my rent.'

'Yes, of course I will. You are helping us so much!'

Kadir asked, 'But why don't you have the address of the babu?'

Sukumar was caught off guard. He somehow made something up, 'My dumb friend lost the paper where this kind man had written down his address. Hence, all the confusion.' Saptarshi smiled weakly in response, pretending to be ashamed of his mistake.

Kadir agreed to take Sukumar and Saptarshi to the place where he had dropped Ram.

'Did the babu and the man from the jewellery shop speak in Bengali?' asked Sukumar.

A rather miffed Kadir remarked, 'You talk too much, brother. The person who needs help is quiet, but you are asking questions like a daroga.'

Suppressing his laughter, Saptarshi feebly pleaded, 'Please help, Kadir bhai!'

'Hahaha!' laughed Kadir. 'The worker from the shop was speaking in Hindi. I think he was a Marwari. The babu was a Bengali bhadralok!'

Sukumar and Saptarshi learnt that Ram had been to Kadir's office to make an advance payment for the horse carriages a day prior to visiting Pal Jewellers. He had provided an address to Sajid for next day's pick-up. Kadir informed them that he had picked up Ram babu from that address and dropped him at Pal Jewellers in Burra Bazar. Rani ji had also been picked-up from the same address and she had been travelling in Sajid's coach. On their way back, Kadir had dropped Ram babu and Deen Dayal at the same address but he wasn't sure where Sajid had dropped Rani ji aka Trinoyoni. Kadir further added that there had been no zamindar in any of the carriages.

As Sukumar and Saptarshi got inside Kadir's carriage, Sukumar asked, 'Couldn't you catch even a glimpse of Rani ji, sitting inside the other coach?'

Kadir replied, 'No, brother. That carriage was not like the one you are sitting in right now. It was fully covered and luxurious...rich people travel in those carriages. You won't understand.' Sukumar nodded, satisfied with Kadir's reasoning.

After travelling for almost half an hour, Sukumar raised his voice to ask Kadir how much further they had to go.

Kadir stopped the carriage almost immediately. The two undercover policemen looked out from the carriage. Kadir pointed to a double-storey house, and smiled, 'That's the house. Hope you get back your job.'

Sukumar and Saptarshi quickly got out of the carriage. After paying Kadir and thanking him for saving Saptarshi's destitute family, they walked up to the house. Unfortunately, it was locked. Sukumar found a notice stuck on the gate that read, 'House to let. Contact the stationery shop opposite to this house for details.'

Sukumar inquired about the house at the stationery shop.

'A rich man had rented it. He owned a huge horse-drawn carriage. But I think he left the house,' said the shopkeeper.

Saptarshi collected the address of the owner from the shop.

'Let's go meet the owner right now then?' Saptarshi asked.

'Wait...look at yourself,' Sukumar reminded him. 'Nobody will rent a mansion to a coachman! We need to come back tomorrow, dressed as Bengali bhadralok.'

The Daroga in Pursuit

The next morning, Sukumar and Saptarshi met the landlord of the house in traditional attire as rich Bengali men and expressed an interest in renting the house. However, the landlord explained that though the house was empty, a rich man had already paid a month's advance and rented the house.

'The gentleman who rented this house left within a few days and hasn't returned yet. But since he has paid me in advance, I have to wait for at least ten more days before I can rent it out again,' the landlord said. 'Can you come back after ten days? The rent would be fifty rupees a month.'

Sukumar said, 'Sure, money is not a problem and I can wait for ten days. But since I am here already, may I take a quick look around the house? My wife will also be coming so—'

The landlord interrupted him and said, 'Oh yes, of course! Please come.' The man was all too happy to show prospective renters around the property.

Sukumar and Saptarshi entered the house with the landlord. It was a big house, a typical bonedi baari. Sukumar stepped into the *thakur dalaan*. There were multiple rooms on both the floors and Sukumar was impatient to scan each one of them. As he was about to step inside the first room, the landlord said, 'Pardon me, but I cannot allow you to go inside the rooms. The existing tenant's family has their belongings here. We cannot enter without their permission. You will get a feel of the house from the courtyard itself.'

Sukumar and Saptarshi exchanged glances and decided to investigate the house later.

'By the way, if you happen to meet your tenant, will you recognize him?' asked Sukumar.

The landlord gave Sukumar a surprised look, 'Of course! Why do you ask?'

'I am asking because I really like the house. If you meet your tenant, perhaps you could check if he can vacate the house before the agreed date? If that is possible, I mean.' Sukumar reasoned weakly, but by now the entire plot was clear to him, so it felt less necessary to keep up an act.

The landlord nodded.

Sukumar stepped out of the house and rushed to Ram and Trinoyoni's house.

'But why are we going there now?' Saptarshi asked on the way.

'I have a hunch that the miscreants will flee if we don't catch them now!' replied Sukumar.

'But what about Deen Dayal Singh then?' Saptarshi asked inquisitively.

Sukumar threw him a curt look and ignored his question.

When Sukumar reached Trinoyoni's house, Ram was standing at the door with a heavy shopping bag containing fish and other items.

'Looks like there is a feast at your house today?' Sukumar smirked.

Ram's heart skipped a beat as he saw the two policemen. But hiding his fear, he replied, 'My son was ill for a few days. He is better now and wanted to have fish rice. So, I bought some fresh fish from the market. Please come in, daroga babu. Join us for lunch. Have you made any headway in the jewellery case?'

Ram walked in as Trinoyoni opened the door. From the look in his eyes, she knew something was wrong. The two policemen followed Ram inside.

'Well, yes! We have got a warrant issued against Deen Dayal. There is no doubt that he stole the jewellery. But till we find him, I would need your support, Ram babu,' stated Sukumar, trying to read Ram and Trinoyoni's expressions. He knew he had to continue his performance in order to keep the two from growing suspicious.

Ram and Trinoyoni exchanged brief relieved glances.

Handing the shopping bag to Trinoyoni, Ram said, 'Of course! That is my duty. If Deen Dayal has stolen the money, he should be punished.'

'Please have lunch with us today, daroga babu,' offered Trinoyoni.

'Ah, thank you very much, Trinoyoni Debi. But we have some urgent work to finish today,' Sukumar replied apologetically.

'We also need to take the zamindar's statement,' said Saptarshi. 'Can you take us to his house, Ram babu?'

'He has left for his home, somewhere in East Bengal, I believe?' fumbled Ram babu.

'But didn't you say he came from outside of Bengal?' asked Sukumar.

'No, I didn't,' Ram babu said aggressively. 'I can show you the house he was staying in. But I don't know where he is now.'

Sukumar understood Ram babu's urge to identify the house and played along.

'That would be very helpful. Can we go right now, please? I would request Trinoyoni Debi to join us too.'

'Oh, but I have so much work around the house to finish,' Trinoyoni pleaded, trying to escape the situation.

'I understand. But we would appreciate your help. This is a critical case, as you can see. Besides, the zamindar babu knows you. He doesn't know Ram babu,' Sukumar said.

'But I told you just now that the zamindar is not in Calcutta! Trinoyoni doesn't need to go to his house!' Ram said authoritatively.

Sukumar tried to keep his calm and politely added, 'Fine then. If you are not willing to help the police, my superiors might suspect you. More police officials will visit your house for questioning. If they drag both of you to the police station, please don't blame me!'

'Okay, okay, I will come. After all, we haven't done anything wrong,' Trinoyoni replied confidently.

Soon, the policemen along with Ram and Trinoyoni started for the zamindar's house. By then, Sukumar was sure that Ram was talking about a fictitious, non-existent zamindar.

After walking for about ten minutes, Ram stopped and pointed towards a house.

'That's the house the zamindar was staying in,' he said. 'Can we leave now?'

'No, wait,' instructed Sukumar.

In the meantime, Saptarshi walked up to the security guard standing outside the house. The guard promptly addressed Saptarshi's queries, as though he had rehearsed the answers. Saptarshi immediately reported his observations to Sukumar adding that the house actually belonged to a zamindar.

'Daroga babu, did the guard confirm that zamindar babu is not in Calcutta?' Ram asked nervously.

Sukumar nodded.

'I would like to leave now, daroga babu. As you know, my son will be eating fish after a long time today,' Ram said, comforted that his security guard friend had conveyed to the police exactly what Ram had instructed him to say.

'I will also join you for lunch, Ram babu. But before that, I want both of you to accompany me to another house. My team has been working on the case all night and they have given me the address of a house where Deen Dayal's brother is working. Maybe he can give us some details on Deen Dayal?' advised Sukumar.

'But...' Ram started.

Sensing his discomfort, Sukumar said, 'I know you have closely interacted with Deen Dayal. My assumption is that the man who stays in that house is an imposter. He is actually Deen Dayal disguised as his own brother. You both can help us nab the culprit!'

Trinoyoni and Ram looked at each other cluelessly.

'Okay, we will come with you,' Ram finally said.

On the way, Sukumar asked, 'Ram babu, the brokerage money you received after selling the jewellery to the zamindar, was it in the form of notes or coins?'

Perplexed, Ram replied, 'How can a wealthy zamindar roam around with coins, daroga babu? Of course, they were currency notes. I had even shared the numbers with you.' Ram and Trinoyoni had started to sweat by now. They knew that the daroga had discovered something he was not ready to reveal to them just yet.

'Oh, yes, I remember,' Sukumar said. 'Do you know that from the currency office, if people have to exchange money, they need to sign on the notes they submit?'

'Yes, I am aware of that,' Ram confirmed.

'Then you will be happy to know that we traced the fraudster Deen Dayal based on the name and address he scribbled on the notes that he submitted to the currency office! Foolish man, he had no clue that we would trace him so easily,' Sukumar lied.

'Oh, really?' Ram gulped. 'Which address did he mention in the notes?'

'Ah, there. That's the house. That's the address we got from the notes,' Sukumar said, with a wicked smile.

Trinoyoni and Ram's jaws dropped as they stood in front of the house. It was the same house that Ram had rented with a month's advance payment. It was the same house that Sukumar and Saptarshi had visited earlier that morning but the landlord had barred them from entering the rooms.

As soon as Sukumar and Saptarshi reached the gate of the house, a few policemen also arrived at the scene. Trinoyoni and Ram looked at them, appalled. The landlord arrived too.

'Arrey...you are in luck, Sukumar babu,' said the landlord. 'You have the current tenant of my house with you. Did he agree to vacate the house?'

'Yes, lucky me,' mocked Sukumar. 'Come in, Ram babu!'

Ram felt his throat dry up. He sheepishly walked in with Trinoyoni. They had been caught. It was no use resisting now.

'Does the house look the same as you left it, Ram babu? Why did you rent this house, by the way?' Saptarshi asked, surprised.

'I...I had to rent it on behalf of the zamindar babu,' Ram managed to say, although now his heart wasn't in the performance.

'But the guard in the other house told us that the zamindar babu was too conscious of his status to even think of renting a house. He owns three houses in Calcutta already!' Sukumar's trap had worked, and this was just play-acting for the sake of it. Everyone was just waiting for an admission of guilt.

'The guard is dumb. The zamindar rented this house as he wanted a secluded place to enjoy the company of his new mistress,' Trinoyoni pitched in, trying her best to cook up an impromptu story.

'Tell me something Trinoyoni Debi, this man...Deen Dayal Singh. Is he a Bengali?' asked Sukumar.

'No, his mother tongue was Hindi,' replied Trinoyoni.

'Was meaning? Is he not alive?' charged Sukumar.

'I...I mean his mother tongue is Hindi,' Trinoyoni said nervously.

'Can he speak in Bengali?' asked Sukumar.

Ram interrupted. 'She hasn't interacted with him much.

Deen Dayal cannot speak Bengali and he has difficulty even understanding the language. I had to speak in broken Hindi to keep the conversation going.'

'I see. That means he cannot write in Bengali too, right?'

Even in that tense situation, Ram laughed. 'I think you have not slept well, daroga babu. I am telling you that Deen Dayal cannot speak in Bengali. How will he write in that language?'

'Thank you for clearing all my doubts Ram babu,' said Sukumar.

In the meantime, the policemen had entered the house and, as instructed by Saptarshi, they were searching for Deen Dayal.

'Look in every nook and corner,' Saptarshi instructed.

'Ram babu, you won't believe what I found at the currency office when I went there to cross check on Deen Dayal!'

Ram was sweating. He rubbed the sweat off his forehead and looked at Sukumar, puzzled.

'I checked the notes Deen Dayal had exchanged. Each note had his name and address written in clean Bengali, without any spelling mistakes. I asked the officer-in-charge if someone had helped him write it. He vehemently denied and said that Deen Dayal spoke in clean Bengali without any Hindi accent and wrote everything himself,' Sukumar said, his gaze not flinching from Ram even for a second.

Ram was furious. 'Why are you telling me all this, daroga babu?'

'Because the man who signed the notes was not a tall, lanky, elderly man with grey hair, the British official confirmed.

He was a middle-aged, pleasant-looking Bengali man with a pocketful of cigars!' Sukumar replied emphatically.

'So?' Ram asked.

'You signed the notes. Not Deen Dayal. You stole the money!' Sukumar said, looking straight into Ram's eyes.

Ram turned red. Trinoyoni didn't utter a word.

'Daroga babu, come here please!' The urgency in Saptarshi's voice caught Sukumar's attention and he rushed to the small garden on the ground floor.

'Take good care of my guests,' Sukumar told the constables, pointing at Ram and Trinoyoni.

Sukumar entered and saw flies and bees crowding the floor.

'This is an unusual amount of flies, even for a garden,' said Saptarshi, disconcerted. 'I cannot understand why!'

'Dig the area up immediately. Continue digging till you find what the bees are after,' Sukumar ordered, furious. He had a hunch that this was a crime scene. The police officials found a shovel to dig the floor in the garden outside the house.

'Isn't it surprising Ram babu, that this axe, extra mud and all the stuff needed to dig and cover the ground is available in this house itself! Looks like someone needed it more than we need it now,' Sukumar mused.

Trinoyoni and Ram sat quietly, surrounded by the policemen in the inner courtyard.

Some policemen started digging the floor. After a while, a filthy pungent smell filled the room, making it difficult for people to breathe. The expressions on the policemen's faces, who were familiar with this smell, changed as they realized the true nature of the crime.

'Keep digging,' shouted Sukumar, covering his nose with his hand, anger rising inside him.

Trinoyoni and Ram looked pale.

After plenty of digging, when the smell was unbearable, a decaying dead body of a tall man was recovered. Unfortunately, the face was distorted and the body so badly damaged that the person was unidentifiable. However, the clothes on the body were intact.

Sukumar and Saptarshi had no doubt that they had retrieved the body of the elderly employee from the jewellery shop—Deen Dayal Singh.

As the police removed the body from the room, the jewellery shop owner arrived.

'Oh my God! What have they done to Deen Dayal?' Gokul Chandra Pal cried, aghast.

Trinoyoni and Ram were still in shock. They were taken into police custody.

On the way, Ram whispered to Trinoyoni, 'Promise me, no matter what happens to me, you will not open your mouth. Nobody should know that you were party to this crime!'

Trinoyoni was crying softly.

'Manik will not survive if both of us go to jail. Please Trinoyoni, promise me you will never leave my son. I don't have time.' Ram had teared up too, realizing that this was the end.

Finally, Trinoyoni managed to utter, 'Yes.'

In police custody, Trinoyoni kept a straight face and denied knowing anything about the crime.

'I knew you were a fraud the day I met you. What about that woman, Trinoyoni? What part did she play in this?' Sukumar asked Ram.

'She doesn't know anything. She is just an innocent courtesan,' Ram tried to convince Sukumar.

Ram was interrogated in police custody for over a week and badly beaten up. Still, he didn't confess to murdering Deen Dayal. Sukumar tried to prise the truth out of him by questioning him every day after he had thoroughly received enough kicks and punches.

'How did you pull off this crime? Tell me, I am dying to know!' coaxed Sukumar, once again. He grabbed Ram's bloodied face by the hair and looked into his eyes, 'If you cooperate, I will try and convert your death sentence into prison time.'

After several days of bearing police torture, Ram decided to break the silence when Sukumar tried to bribe him by saying that he would save him from capital punishment.

Ram started with a lot of difficulty since his throat was dry and his lips were swollen, 'I didn't lie to you about the zamindar. Indeed, I met a zamindar who wanted to buy wedding clothes and jewellery from Calcutta for his son's marriage. He had visited several shops but the touts were all out to loot him and he was being mobbed by brokers every time he entered the market. Frustrated, he decided to return to his hometown. Luckily, I met him and offered him an irresistible deal. He bought a lot of clothes from my recommended garment shops. I made good profits. But my objective was to make him buy jewellery and earn more money.' He coughed up blood and asked for water. Sukumar remained unmoved.

Ram continued, 'I understood his requirements and told him that I would arrange for twenty thousand rupees worth of jewellery he was looking for. He paid me a thousand rupees as advance. I could have just fled with that money but my greed ruined me,' heaved Ram.

Ram slowly disclosed his sinister plan to Sukumar, omitting Trinoyoni's involvement completely. He started by telling Sukumar how he had managed to rent the huge mansion.

'I told the owner that a rich zamindar would be visiting Calcutta to shop for a wedding and thus needed the house. I also paid him the full month's rent in advance. Then I asked Trinoyoni to shift to this house with me, posing as a Rani. I also hired two carriages from the office near the house and selected the horses myself. The carriages were parked outside the house so that people would notice that a wealthy family resided there. Some people saw Trinoyoni leaving in the carriage. When we reached the jewellery store, I got off from my vehicle but Trinoyoni remained seated inside hers. I took the jewellery items to her and she selected the ones the zamindar would like to purchase.'

'And she didn't know about your evil plan?' Sukumar narrowed his eyes.

Ram vigorously shook his head. He had decided to lie to keep Trinoyoni and Manik safe.

'Okay, what happened next?' The daroga lit a cigar and sat back.

'Trinoyoni told me that she had selected the jewellery.

She asked me to send them to the zamindar, who would then pay me in cash. Then she left in her carriage,' claimed Ram as he looked at the smoke, pining for a drag.

'But didn't she question you about why you needed to shift to this rented place when you already have a house of your own?' asked Sukumar. He knew that Ram was protecting her. He wanted to incriminate both of them—that would solve the crime. Arresting Ram was just half of it.

'No, she didn't question me because she loves me very much and obeys me. I told her that she had to serve the zamindar for a few days and so she willingly shifted to this house. I knew that the zamindar would never visit. But she wasn't aware,' Ram lied again.

'Later, I went to that rented house along with Deen Dayal. His job was to deliver the jewellery to the zamindar, collect the payment, pay me my brokerage and leave. I asked Deen Dayal to come inside the house with me to get his money. As Deen Dayal walked in, I asked him to give me the jewellery first. He refused to give it to me before receiving the money. I hit him with a brass bucket and he fell to the floor. I sat on his chest and strangled him to death. After that, I dug the ground and buried him right there. Then I covered the floor with lots of mud and garbage. Well, you know the rest of the story,' concluded Ram.

'What a monster you are!' fumed Sukumar. 'You did all this alone?' He still wasn't convinced by Ram's story. There was no way that Trinoyoni wasn't involved.

Ram babu lied again. 'Yes, I don't need an accomplice. I didn't want to share my money.'

What Ram didn't tell Sukumar was that when Deen Dayal

had reached the rented house with him, Trinoyoni had been waiting inside. She had tried to seduce Deen Dayal and asked him, 'Show me all the jewellery you have got!'

Deen Dayal had refused and apologized, 'Pardon me Rani ji. I have to see the money first. There has been a lot of fraud in our area in the last month.'

Ram had angrily pushed Deen Dayal. 'Is this the way to behave with a rani? What do you think of yourself, old man?'

Deen Dayal had folded his hands and said, 'I am sorry if I insulted you. I don't want to sell the jewellery here. Kindly excuse me.'

As he had prepared to leave, Ram had flung his shoe at Deen Dayal with such force that it had hit the elderly man on his chest, hurting him badly.

Suddenly, Ram had begun kicking Deen Dayal. Nervous, the old man had fallen to the ground and began choking. Ram had pulled him down, sprung up on his chest and pressed his feet on Deen Dayal's neck. The harmless man couldn't even move! This is when Trinoyoni had leapt forward and started kicking Deen Dayal's face with all her might. Deen Dayal had been shocked as he had never witnessed such an aggressive and ruthless woman. When he had made a desperate attempt to free his neck from Ram's feet with his two hands, Trinoyoni had assaulted him further. She had moved his hands back and twisted them so badly that he became immobile. Then she had gripped Deen Dayal's feet with her whole body, so that he stayed paralysed while Ram violently pressed his neck with his feet. Finally, Deen Dayal had not been able to resist the attack anymore and succumbed to his assailants.

Ram knew that he wouldn't have succeeded in killing

Deen Dayal without Trinoyoni's help. The duo had become seasoned criminals now. They hadn't felt guilt even for a split second after seeing Deen Dayal's lifeless body. Instead, they had rushed to open the jewellery boxes to verify if Deen Dayal had brought all the jewellery that had been ordered. Trinoyoni's eyes had sparkled as she looked at the shiny gold and gems, and seeing that their financial problems were finally at an end, she had forgotten all about Deen Dayal's corpse in front of her.

'We have been so worried. It's been ages since we enjoyed so freely!' Trinoyoni had said.

'You are right,' Ram had replied, stroking Trinoyoni's tresses gently. 'Now, let's get rid of the dead body!'

'Oh, we can just drag and throw the man in the street, like we did with the young boys we intoxicated some years back,' Trinoyoni had suggested.

'No, it won't be so easy. People might see us. Besides, if police find the body, they will first come to us. We have to think differently this time,' Ram had argued.

'Why not bury the body in the room where it is lying?'

'You are brilliant. We will do exactly that,' Ram had responded. They had slowly walked to the next room where Deen Dayal's dead body lay staring at them.

'Close his eyes. I feel scared,' Trinoyoni had said. Ram had tried to close the eyes but Deen Dayal's corpse had become stiff.

'We've lost time. Let's quickly bury it now. The police have set up a new detective department. I don't want those obnoxious darogas coming here, sniffing out a crime.' Saying this, Ram had dragged the body to the garden, where he had stocked a shovel, mud and other material. Trinoyoni had been surprised to find that Ram had already made all the arrangements.

The criminals had spent hours digging the soft mud in the garden. Finally, Ram and Trinoyoni had pulled Deen Dayal's body and dropped it into the big hole they had dug. Then they had tried their best to cover up the hole. The level of the ground however, remained uneven. They had decided to cover it up with garbage.

'Let it be,' Ram had said. 'By the time anyone finds the body, we will be long gone. The body will be decomposed and unidentifiable by then.'

Then, Trinoyoni and Ram had returned to their room, packed all their things and left, as if nothing had happened.

The next morning, Ram had sold the jewellery to the zamindar at a premium price.

⁓∞⁓

As Ram was immersed in his thoughts, Sukumar nudged him, 'You went to the currency office and signed off as Deen Dayal, right?'

Ram nodded.

'Where is the rest of the money?' Sukumar demanded. The case wasn't done for him. He wanted to recover the money and incriminate Trinoyoni. Otherwise, it was a lost case! Sukumar knew that even though Ram was in police custody, he hadn't solved the puzzle yet.

'I don't know. Most of it was spent paying off debts,' Ram lied.

He couldn't tell Sukumar that he had handed over all the money to Trinoyoni, who had safely hidden it inside a brass jar containing rice.

The police thoroughly searched Trinoyoni's house but were unable to recover the money. She had already buried the money under a tree in her neighbour's garden and nobody had any inkling about it, except Manik. Sukumar tried his best but failed to retrieve the stolen money from Trinoyoni.

Though, initially, both Ram and Trinoyoni had been arrested, due to lack of evidence, Ram's notorious accomplice walked free. Neither the people at the jewellery shop nor the owner of the rented house had seen Trinoyoni. Although, some people in the neighbourhood and the charioteer of her horse-drawn carriage had seen Rani ji. However, Trinoyoni had been covered in make-up, expensive clothes and jewellery in her avatar as Rani ji. Besides, her face had remained hidden under the veil. Thus, nobody recognized Trinoyoni as Rani ji. Sukumar had no option but to release her from police custody.

However, everyone recognized Ram. The currency officer remembered Ram very well and identified him as Deen Dayal. The magistrate lodged a theft and murder case against Ram and sent the case for trial.

Once Trinoyoni was out of jail, she tried her best to save her dearest Ram babu. She begged many people to help her. However, no one came forward to help. Instead, they cheated her and extracted a lot of money from her.

Trinoyoni paid handsomely to hire a lawyer. All her money and valuables gathered through their fradulent schemes was spent fighting Ram's case. She also dug out the money hidden in her neighbour's garden to fight the case. Trinoyoni even bribed detectives and bought fake witnesses. However, all her efforts were in vain. Ram's case went to court and the jury found him guilty on multiple accounts. He was sentenced to death.

She remembered Ram's last words. 'Forgive me, Trinoyoni. You drained your life's savings taking care of me and trying to save me. Forgive me for turning you into a criminal.'

Trinoyoni promised Ram that she would never abandon Manik, come what may. Before they parted ways forever, Ram told her, 'It's true that we will not be meeting anymore in this life, Trinoyoni. But we will meet again in the next birth. I will pray to God that he gives me a guilt-free life, a life of love and fulfilment with my true love—Trinoyoni. I have only loved you this entire rotten life of mine.'

Ram began crying. Trinoyoni promised to reunite with him in heaven and to be his wife every time she was reborn on earth. She clearly remembered Ram's sullen face when he bid her goodbye. His last words were, '*Bidaay priyotoma. Abar dekha hobe* (Farewell my beloved. We will meet again).'

As the guard pulled Ram away, Trinoyoni started walking out, crying uncontrollably. The other prisoners and their visitors thought that Ram was her husband, and, in a way, he was. Even if they had never been married, Ram was Trinoyoni's husband. There was no other way they could define their relationship.

Trinoyoni didn't know what to do next. So far, to fight

her battles and to execute all criminal activities, she had had Ram's unflinching support. How would she survive now? She had exhausted all her money, down to the last dime.

Life after Ram Babu

The trial and execution of Ram babu shattered Trinoyoni and she remained listless and unresponsive for weeks. During these trying times, not a single soul stood by her. All the people Trinoyoni had worked with in the past, including Narayan, who had teamed up with her and Ram to organize fake marriages, disappeared from her life.

Trinoyoni was almost destitute. All her wealth had been drained fighting Ram's case. She had sold off all her jewellery and even mortgaged her house. The only person Trinoyoni could call her own was Ram's son Manik, whose upbringing was her responsibility now. Trinoyoni was forced to sell her palatial house just to put food on the table.

Trinoyoni moved into a small rented house in a slum area. Even so, she did not have enough money after she paid the advance and purchased some necessities. She defaulted in paying the rent and the landlord threatened to throw her out. For survival, she decided to resume sleeping with customers. But she was too poor to afford new clothes or any jewellery. She didn't have the money to even wash her hair properly. She decided to chop off her thick knee-length mane and sell it at a decent price, which allowed her to buy some clothes and imitation jewellery. Manik was very upset to see his mother with short hair, but Trinoyoni assured him that it would grow back.

The middle-aged Trinoyoni made a desperate attempt to attract men. The years of crime and living in near poverty with Ram had taken a toll on her. Unable to afford the luxury of servants and coachmen, she had to do most things herself, which made her skin rough. The short hair, the clothes and fake jewellery made matters worse. Wealthy men were not interested in her anymore and the ones she had turned down earlier despised her now. The lower caste men who shared her bed for peanuts were mostly labourers and daily-wage earners. They were ruthless in bed and their body odour made Trinoyoni almost retch every time. However, she kept quiet and bore the brunt, only for Manik.

When Trinoyoni decided to sleep with her landlord, she had no clue that it would turn into a nightmare. The deal was that since she was unable to pay the rent, she had to sleep with him thrice a week. Initially, she was hesitant, but when the landlord threatened to throw her out of the house, she had no choice but to agree. It was an ordeal for Trinoyoni because the landlord used to beat her up while indulging in sex. She had bruises all over her body, which she tried her best to hide from Manik and prospective customers.

In the past, Trinoyoni had heard horror stories from her brothel friends about how ill-tempered and possessive customers would sometimes derive sadistic pleasure by beating up their mistresses during sex. While most of the tormented women suffered silently, some of them died, whether accidentally or on purpose, it was never known.

The criminals, however, were never punished. Instead, they boasted to other misogynistic monsters about how they enjoyed enslaving their wives and mistresses.

Trinoyoni thought a lot about other odd-jobs she could take up in order to feed Manik. However, she knew nobody would employ her as a housemaid because of her Sonagachi association. At times, she reminisced how she and Ram had cheated people and thought that this was God's way of punishing her for her innumerable sins. However, she was mature enough to understand that if she spent any more time regretting the past, her future would get shrouded in darkness.

Her only way out of the miseries was to get back into the world of crime. But this time, she would have to do everything on her own. Soon, Trinoyoni's criminal mind began hatching new plots and exploring new crimes far more dangerous than anything she had attempted before. And every time she would back away from an idea, a look at Manik's face would steel her resolve. She had to do it for him.

The Spiritual Guru

'Where are we going so early in the morning, mother?' Manik asked, as Trinoyoni almost dragged him out of bed before sunrise.

'We are going to your aunt's house,' Trinoyoni replied hurriedly.

'Which aunt? All my relatives are aunties. I don't want to go to Sonagachi,' Manik pleaded and started sniffling.

Trinoyoni hugged him, her heart breaking a little to see him cry, 'Aren't you my good boy? Please listen to me. I have to meet my friend Kumkum urgently. I had a nightmare that she is in trouble. If I don't go, I won't get peace of mind.'

Manik never disobeyed his foster mother; he quickly got up from the bed.

When Trinoyoni and Manik reached the Sonagachi brothel, they learnt that Kumkum had left the main house and moved to a small hut in a nearby slum. Trinoyoni was able to find Kumkum's house quite easily among the sea of shanties.

Trinoyoni hugged Kumkum and said, 'I am so happy to see you, dear sister. It's been over six months. I am sorry I couldn't visit you earlier.'

To her surprise, Kumkum didn't seem excited to meet Trinoyoni. Earlier, the girl used to be overjoyed by Trinoyoni's presence. Trinoyoni could sense that Kumkum was not her usual self. She seemed morose and indifferent.

As Kumkum served water with a face devoid of any expression, Trinoyoni said, 'I had to run to you my dear sister. I had a nightmare last night that you were in deep trouble. My heart was shattered. I knew I had to meet you today itself. Ask Manik how worried I was!'

Manik nodded as Trinoyoni looked at him for validation. Kumkum remained quiet.

Trinoyoni clasped her hands and asked, 'Is everything okay, dear sister?'

Suddenly, Kumkum started crying. Trinoyoni held her closer.

In between her sobs, Kumkum kept repeating, 'I am finished, didi. I have nothing left in life. I just want to die.'

'Oh, I wish I was dead before you uttered those words. My sister is in so much pain and I came to meet her so late! Oh, please tell me what is wrong?' Trinoyoni pleaded, sounding concerned, as she brought Kumkum's head closer to her chest.

Kumkum wiped her tears and sniffled, 'I don't know what to tell you! I had so much money and so many men running after me. Now I have nothing.'

'Wh-what happened?' Trinoyoni kept nudging Kumkum to reveal the real issue. She gently rubbed Kumkum's neck and back, consoling her.

'Manik, why don't you go out and play for a while,' Trinoyoni urged, sensing that Kumkum wasn't comfortable confiding in her with Manik around.

As Manik stepped out, Kumkum said, 'I was with a very good babu for a long time. He showered all his riches on me and pampered me endlessly. But my greed was increasing day by day and I demanded whatever I wanted. I named it and he fetched it for me. I was very proud. Why wouldn't I be? I was the centre of attraction and stories of my beauty spread far and wide. I had so many other babus dying to meet me and drown me in riches and jewellery. They lured me with exorbitantly priced jewellery and clothing. But I couldn't accept anything as I was the good babu's "kept" woman. He scolded me one day threatening, "You are only mine. If you look at someone else, I will slit your throat."'

'Oh my God! What happened next?' Trinoyoni asked, appalled at the babu's behaviour.

Kumkum replied, 'I felt I could earn a lot more if I left this babu. He had been like God to me. But I wanted to get rid of him so that I could enjoy other luxuries. So, one day, I just kicked him out of my house. I misbehaved with him and asked him to never come back again! He left, enraged.'

'Oh no! Did you get a better customer after that?' Trinoyoni asked impatiently.

'Huh! It was as though I had asked Goddess Lakshmi to leave my home. All my wealth vanished with my beloved babu's departure.' Tears ran down Kumkum's face again.

'What happened to all those men waiting for you?' Trinoyoni asked, surprised.

'No one came,' Kumkum cried out. 'Not a single person came to my house after my babu left. All that mirage of riches, jewellery and money was gone. A friend told me that stories of my misbehaviour had spread everywhere. Customers stopped visiting, as they didn't want to be insulted by a prostitute.'

Kumkum paused to drink some water.

'Then what happened, my friend?' asked Trinoyoni.

'One night, I was so exhausted pleading with rich men to hire me that I fell asleep outside my house, on the road. When I woke up, I realized that I was…I was being raped by two beggars,' Kumkum gripped Trinoyoni's hands tightly as she confided her deepest secret in her.

'I froze in fear. They left me after they had had enough of me. I couldn't talk to anybody about it. Policemen would laugh at me. Once, a police babu, who was my customer, had told me that a beshya has no honour and she cannot be raped.' Kumkum wailed as the memory played in her mind.

Trinoyoni hugged Kumkum, her heart sinking with pain.

Kumkum continued, 'Since then, beggars sit outside my home at night, laughing wickedly and begging to sleep with me for free!'

'Did you try contacting your old babu?' Trinoyoni asked. 'What if he has had a change of heart and wants to accept you as his mistress again?'

Kumkum covered her face with her hands and cried. 'Yes, I tried every possible way to bring him back but he never returned. I went to his house also. But he kicked me out. He threatened to kill me if I tried to contact him again.'

'How long have you been in pain like this, my dear?' asked Trinoyoni.

'I have stopped counting the days. I have no money left and I was forced to sell more than half of my jewellery. I used to have such a large collection! You remember, don't you, didi?' Kumkum asked.

Trinoyoni remembered. She had seen Kumkum a few times after she and Ram babu had turned to crime. She had been jealous of Kumkum and her jewellery then. 'Yes, I do. You had some spectacular jewellery indeed. I wish you had told me about your unbearable pain earlier, dear sister. I could have helped you. I still can! Not only will you get back your lost wealth, your babu will come back to you too!'

Kumkum was amazed at Trinoyoni's statement. 'Oh didi! You are very kind and doing everything to console me. I appreciate your help. But please don't give me false hope,' she said, a tad offended as reality hit her.

'I am not giving you any false hope, Kumkum,' Trinoyoni stated confidently.

Kumkum's eyes widened with the new hope that Trinoyoni was dangling in front of her. She suddenly jumped off the bed and grabbed Trinoyoni's feet with both hands. She rubbed her head against Trinoyoni's feet and howled, 'Please help me, didi! Else, I will die.'

Trinoyoni quickly pulled Kumkum up. 'Look at me straight now. Sit here.' Kumkum did as instructed.

'Now listen to me carefully,' Trinoyoni said, clearing her throat.

'I know a Gurudeb who has come down from heaven only to help people in distress. He is a spiritual guru, always dressed in white. His hair, beard, moustache...everything is milky white. I don't know how old he is but people believe he is more than a hundred years old. But he looks like a young sadhu. His knowledge and wisdom are unmatched. I am fortunate that he has agreed to make me his *shishya*. My master is a true saint. He is an incarnation of God on earth. Perhaps, he is God. I don't know. All I know is that when I was in distress, Gurudeb rescued me and now I have my health, wealth and riches—all back in place,' Trinoyoni blatantly lied.

'Oh my God! How did it happen, didi?' Kumkum asked, awestruck.

Trinoyoni continued, 'If Gurudeb is impressed, he will do everything for his disciples. He can remove all obstacles and poverty from people's lives and restore happiness. He can wipe out all the pain from your life. But do you know the best thing that my Gurudeb does?'

Eyes all lit up, Kumkum asked, 'What?'

Trinoyoni took a deep breath, 'He will double your wealth and jewellery if he is impressed with you!'

Then, to add some more meat to her story, Trinoyoni continued, 'I met a few other girls last week. They had lost everything. I introduced them to Gurudeb and he blessed them wholeheartedly. After his meditation, Gurudeb sprinkled holy water on them and whispered his magic mantra in their ears. And then...' Trinoyoni paused.

'Then what happened, didi?' Kumkum asked, wide-eyed.

'The girls went home and continued to recite his mantra and eat the prasad. Slowly and steadily, their financial condition improved and they became rich. Since then, they have remained dedicated followers of my Gurudeb.'

From the look on Kumkum's face, Trinoyoni knew that the naïve girl had believed her tale and was dying to meet the fictitious Gurudeb. Her excitement was evident in her restlessness.

Before Trinoyoni could say anything else, Kumkum held Trinoyoni's hands and implored, 'Oh didi! I wish you had told me about your divine Gurudeb earlier. Can you please introduce me to him? You can see my condition. I want to seek his blessings. Please help me.'

Kumkum got up from her bed and started pulling Trinoyoni. 'Please take me to him now, I beg of you!'

Calmly, Trinoyoni replied, 'That is not possible. Gurudeb doesn't like to meet strangers just like that. He will get angry and leave. This is not a good time to meet him.'

Kumkum started nagging. 'Please, I want to meet him. How much money does he charge? I will pay more. Should I cook something for him? Please tell me didi, don't keep quiet.'

Now that a door had been opened for her, Kumkum wanted to know everything. She wanted her life back. Trinoyoni knew that look of desperation. She had Kumkum exactly where she wanted her.

Trinoyoni said, 'Come here and sit down first.' Kumkum obliged.

'Now close your eyes and breathe gently. Listen to what I say patiently. Do not interrupt.'

Kumkum followed Trinoyoni's instructions. Trinoyoni began talking slowly and calmly.

'Gurudeb doesn't meet people just like that. He has his own rules. Don't even think of gifting him any cash, food or anything else. He is not materialistic. He might get offended and refuse to see you again. I have never seen him eat or sleep. He only meditates.'

'Oh, what a saintly man,' Kumkum reacted, folding her hands.

Then, Trinoyoni lowered her voice and said, 'I know you are excited to hear about Gurudeb. But please be careful not to discuss him with your friends. If everyone starts visiting him, Gurudeb's meditation might get disrupted and he might head back to the mountains. So, this is all secret information. Understood?'

Kumkum nodded vehemently and said, 'And if too many people know about his magical powers, the charm might get lost too, right?'

Trinoyoni nodded.

'When can I meet him then?' asked Kumkum.

'Gurudeb doesn't stay here. He meditates at a far-off place in a secluded garden. Let us meet him day after tomorrow. I cannot guarantee that he will meet you. But we can try. Do you know the pond at Manicktola?' Trinoyoni asked.

'The big one?'

Trinoyoni nodded. 'Meet me there an hour before sunrise. Make sure you come alone. Then, we will walk together towards his holy abode. I will also sneak out of my house quietly. If Manik wakes up, he won't let me go.'

Kumkum said. 'Thank you, didi! I will reach on time. I will be ever grateful to you.'

'Oh, and yes,' added Trinoyoni, almost like an afterthought. 'I forgot to mention an important fact. The first time you meet Gurudeb, he will bless you with his magic words. He will say, "May the jewellery you are wearing be doubled." This blessing always comes true. So, whether you are wearing just one piece of jewellery or twenty pieces, the number will double after he blesses you. When I met him for the first time, I wasn't wearing enough ornaments. After he blessed me, I went home and was elated to discover that I had two identical pieces of each jewellery item that I had been wearing! I couldn't believe my eyes. Since you are in such dire need of money, my dear sister, check what you wear carefully before you meet him. If there is one gold chain, it will become two. Two chains will become four. So, select your ornaments intelligently.' Trinoyoni was sure to spell out this last bit of information as slowly as possible, so that every word and gesture would impress itself upon Kumkum. She looked at Kumkum closely.

'Yes didi, I understand,' Kumkum replied excitedly.

'Day after tomorrow. Manicktola pond,' Trinoyoni repeated before leaving Kumkum's house.

Once back home, Trinoyoni threw herself into planning her latest scheme. This was the first time she was executing a plan all by herself. She closed her eyes, remembered Ram babu and said a silent prayer. Trinoyoni couldn't sleep all night. She kept plotting and planning and re-planning.

She was scared and apprehensive as to what would happen if Kumkum found out that she was being looted. Trinoyoni thought, *If Kumkum learns that I stole her jewellery, I will lose her trust forever. What if she discovers that there is no Gurudeb and that I tried to trap her? What if she goes to the police? What if she tells everyone at Sonagachi that Trinoyoni is a thief?*

Trinoyoni mulled over her plan over and over again. She kept turning in her bed restlessly. She realized that she also needed a place to hide the stolen ornaments. Racking her brains overnight, Trinoyoni finally found a solution. Everything had to be meticulously planned. Only after ensuring that her solution was risk-free was Trinoyoni able to sleep.

The next day, Manik found his mother's behaviour very strange. Trinoyoni was sitting in her room with a fowl and feeding her some leftover food.

Surprised, Manik asked, 'Why have you got a fowl, mother? We don't eat fowl meat.'

Trinoyoni had been so engrossed in planning her mission that she hadn't thought about the questions Manik might ask.

'This...this is Kanan mashi's pet,' she said, referring to her neighbour. 'She asked me to look after her fowl as she is out of town today.'

As soon as Manik left, Trinoyoni stared at the fowl, all energies focused on the animal's weak, long neck. Then all of a sudden, she gripped the helpless fowl's neck and pressed it with both hands with all her might. The fowl cried out in pain, flapping her wings desperately, trying to wriggle free from Trinoyoni's trap. Trinoyoni continued strangling the poor animal. Within a few minutes, the fowl died. Trinoyoni was drenched in sweat. She threw the fowl away as she realized that she was holding on to the dead body.

'This is simpler than I had imagined,' she told herself. She remembered Deen Dayal's lifeless body and how easy it had been to kill him. But that was because Ram babu had been with her. And there had been so much gold! It was the thing that gave her the most joy. Trinoyoni reminded herself to look at the jewellery when she was with Kumkum. It would make the experience more bearable.

She got up to wash her hands. As she turned around, Trinoyoni froze.

Manik was standing right behind her. There was shock written all over his face. He had just witnessed his mother killing a harmless fowl, for reasons unknown to him.

The Serial Killer's First Prey

Trinoyoni woke up very early on the day she was scheduled to meet Kumkum. Like every other day, she took a quick bath and performed her morning prayers. With folded hands, she asked Ma Durga to forgive her for the crime she was going to commit.

Before leaving home, Trinoyoni kept some milk and flattened rice aside for Manik. She knew he would be hungry as soon as he woke up and would demand his regular *dudh-chire*.

Wearing a dull-blue cotton sari, Trinoyoni left home. It was still very dark and she reached the Manicktola pond much ahead of time. To her surprise, Kumkum was already waiting there. She was wearing a cotton sari and had covered herself with a thick shawl.

'My dear sister,' Trinoyoni greeted Kumkum with a smile. 'You have reached very early!'

Kumkum replied, sounding fatigued, 'I reached last night only, didi. I fell asleep sitting behind that big tree,' she said, pointing to a banyan tree near them.

'But why do you have that heavy shawl in this sultry weather? Are you ill?' Trinoyoni asked.

Kumkum looked around and opened the shawl briefly. 'For this,' she whispered, showing Trinoyoni the jewellery that she was wearing. Almost immediately, she covered herself with the shawl again.

Trinoyoni was stunned when she saw the amount of jewellery that Kumkum was wearing! Somehow, she managed to hide her excitement. Kumkum was wearing multiple earrings that covered her ears completely, heavy gold necklaces, arm bands with precious gems embedded in them, gold and silver bangles that covered her hands completely, huge anklets on her feet, rings around all her fingers and toes, a nose pin and a bejewelled tiara on her forehead. There was a gold hairpin in her hair bun too. She was literally covered in gold!

Trinoyoni's mind was racing and she could feel her heart pounding faster with every passing moment. Her hands and feet were cold and she was sweating. She took a deep breath and looked around carefully. It was quiet and completely desolate. There was nobody in the vicinity.

Kumkum interrupted the silence and said, 'I cannot thank you enough. When Gurudeb doubles my wealth, I want to gift you one piece of jewellery. I will have two of each ornament anyway, so you can choose whatever you want,' Kumkum said innocently.

Trinoyoni was finding it hard to breathe and Kumkum's endless chatter was distracting her from her goal.

She managed to collect herself and said, 'No, no, sister. It's your jewellery and Gurudeb will bless you with abundance. I don't want any part of it. He has given me so much already. Now, let's walk towards his meditation area without wasting more time. Follow me.'

Trinoyoni tried her best to avoid eye contact with the naïve Kumkum who tagged along hurriedly, her jewellery jingling as she moved.

The two women started walking briskly over the Manicktola bridge, supposedly towards Trinoyoni's fictitious guru's den. They walked for almost an hour, crossing many houses, gardens and ponds. Finally, they reached a jungle-like place, covered with dense trees and marshland with no hint of habitation around. They walked through that marshland till they reached a pond. Kumkum was thoroughly tired, having walked all this distance with the weight of the jewellery on her.

After resting for a few minutes, Trinoyoni said, 'Sister, the garden where my Gurudeb resides is just around the corner, right behind that cave-like enclosure. He lives inside the cave most of the times and meditates in the garden, away from the public eye.'

Kumkum raised her hands in the air, folded them, closed her eyes and prayed silently. Trinoyoni tried not to get distracted by Kumkum's constant display of faith.

'Gurudeb wants all his disciples to take a dip in this holy pond and purify themselves before meeting him. Then, in their wet clothes, they need to walk to him and seek his blessings,' Trinoyoni informed Kumkum.

'Let's go, didi,' Kumkum said, impatiently. 'But, what about my jewellery?'

Sensing her discomfort, Trinoyoni suggested, 'Remove your jewellery and keep it on the steps leading to the pond. Why spoil it in the water? After purifying yourself with the holy dip, put them back and then meet Gurudeb. You must wear all the ornaments when you meet him.'

Kumkum obeyed Trinoyoni's instructions without a word or any suspicion. She swiftly took off all the jewellery from her body and placed it on the stairs. Then, she held Trinoyoni's hand and gently stepped into the water.

Trinoyoni took a dip holding Kumkum's hand. Kumkum imitated Trinoyoni's action. Then, Trinoyoni requested Kumkum to wipe off the dirt from the back of her neck. Kumkum obliged but mentioned, 'You are clean, didi. There is no dirt on you.'

Then, suddenly, Trinoyoni said, 'Oh, there is something stuck on your back sister. Let me rub it for you.'

As Kumkum turned around, Trinoyoni asked her to lower her head so that the dirt would wash away. Kumkum bent forward and lowered her head with her back to Trinoyoni. With trembling hands, Trinoyoni used all her force to drown Kumkum. Trinoyoni pressed Kumkum's shoulders and head deeper into the water with all her might. Kumkum wriggled in pain, her hands and legs flailing about, waiting to be released. For a moment, she managed to loosen Trinoyoni's grip. Her face underwater and out of breath, she tried to call out to Trinoyoni, but the water muffled her screams.

Trinoyoni was focused on her goal. She remembered the force with which she had killed the innocent fowl at her house. Kumkum managed to pull her head out of the water for a few seconds and screamed hoarsely, 'Why, didi?' But before she could ask her anything else, Trinoyoni gripped her neck with renewed and increased force and tried to push her under the water again.

Kumkum was appalled at Trinoyoni's betrayal and couldn't believe what was happening to her. She tried her best to get out of Trinoyoni's grip, but her strength was no match for Trinoyoni's. Trinoyoni kept applying force and succeeded in pushing Kumkum's head under the water again. Trinoyoni was in complete control. Her body was tense, her teeth gritted in concentration. She had Kumkum where she wanted and had a strong grip around her neck. She looked at the gold jewellery on the steps. The sight seemed to increase the strength in her arms. She doubled her efforts.

Less than a minute later, Kumkum stopped battling. But Trinoyoni kept pressing Kumkum's neck even though she could sense that there was no life left in Kumkum's body. To be sure, she kept Kumkum's head dipped inside the water for some more time. After five more minutes, when her strength was deserting her, Trinoyoni finally released her grip and pushed Kumkum's dead body away.

Then, she slowly walked towards the steps of the pond, panting. She sat down on the steps and surveyed the pond with her eagle eyes. She couldn't see Kumkum's body. Next, she grabbed all of Kumkum's jewellery from the steps and hid them inside her sari and packed the rest in Kumkum's shawl.

Then, she walked back to the main garden and sat down under a banyan tree. Trinoyoni cried her heart out as she remembered Kumkum's last words to her—a sound that would haunt her forever.

When Trinoyoni reached home, Manik was still sleeping. She carefully hid the jewellery in her almirah, trying her best not to wake Manik up. But her arms were still shaking from the deed she had committed, and the jewellery jingled as she put it away. Trinoyoni took a bath, washed her clothes and put on fresh, clean clothes. She spent a lot of time praying that day.

Over the next few days, Trinoyoni sold off all the jewellery one by one and earned a good deal of money that helped her regain her financial stability for some time.

Slowly, Trinoyoni got back to her normal life of interacting with people and sleeping with rich men whenever possible. She couldn't give that up. In addition to a consistent income, it also provided cover for her and would arouse less suspicion among other people. She visited the Sonagachi brothel several times too, just to be sure that nobody was suspecting her for Kumkum's disappearance. One day, Trinoyoni gathered the courage to visit Kumkum's neighbourhood.

She met an old prostitute friend and asked, 'Didi, Kumkum's house is locked. Do you know when she will be back?'

The woman replied, 'Oh, Trinoyoni. Even I am waiting for Kumkum to return. I haven't seen her for several days. She borrowed money from me and never returned.'

Trinoyoni spoke to a few others and learnt that she had borrowed money from many people.

One of Kumkum's neighbours remarked, 'That shameless whore must have gone back to her babu. The way she was begging him, almost ready to dance naked, he must have taken her back.'

Kumkum's next-door neighbour said, 'I think she has ended her own life because she has never disappeared for such a long time. She used to be so depressed. She was having quarrels with our landlord also. The poor girl had no money.'

Trinoyoni sympathized with everyone in the neighbourhood and left. She could now be sure that there was nothing that connected her to Kumkum's death.

A couple of weeks later, while buying vegetables from the market, Trinoyoni overheard a few men engrossed in conversation.

One man said, 'Yes, the police found a dead body in the Manicktola pond.'

A second man said, 'Do they know who the woman was?'

One of them spat out his paan, 'No idea. Must be some whore!'

The first man repeated from the newspaper he was holding, 'The police think it is a case of suicide.'

Trinoyoni understood that the people were discussing Kumkum's death. To everyone else, it was just another prostitute who had killed herself. Then, the three men began joking about the suicide as though the life of a courtesan had no value. Trinoyoni felt a lump in her throat, wondering what kind of death awaited her.

Murder or Suicide?

In mid-1880, almost six months after murdering her friend Kumkum, Trinoyoni was in need of money again. The wealth she had accumulated after selling the stolen jewellery was almost over and she decided to look for her next victim.

This time, Trinoyoni decided to trap middle-aged Bimala, an old acquaintance from Sonagachi, who lived in a small slum in North Calcutta. Bimala had been a popular courtesan in her prime. She had been the mistress of a wealthy zamindar, whose untimely demise had shattered her completely. She had been love with him and couldn't accept his death. She had sunk into depression and by the time she had decided to return to sex work, her customers were not interested in her. She was forced to move out of her Sonagachi brothel, as she couldn't afford to pay the rent anymore. She rented a small room in a slum, trying her best to lure clients, ready to accept any amount of money and sometimes even a plate of rice in exchange for sex.

Trinoyoni took advantage of the fact that Bimala did not know Kumkum. So, she knew it would be easy to deceive Bimala with the same spiritual guru story that had worked with Kumkum. However, and more importantly, Trinoyoni was aware that Bimala loved jewellery so much that she would rather starve for days than consider selling it. Trinoyoni was sure that Bimala had all her jewellery safely hidden somewhere.

One morning, she knocked on Bimala's door.

A haggard-looking Bimala greeted her with a hug. 'Oh, Trinoyoni! How are you, my sister?'

'I am fine, my dear Bimala didi. I had a nightmare that something terrible has happened to you so I rushed to meet you. Hope everything is fine?' Trinoyoni asked, using the same emotional connect she had manufactured with Kumkum.

'I am broke, sister,' Bimala said. 'I have no money and no customers. I just want to die!'

Trinoyoni knew that the time was right to pitch her fictitious Gurudeb to the gullible Bimala.

Consoling her, Trinoyoni commented, 'I was in a similar state a few months back till I met my Gurudeb. He changed my life forever.'

Bimala asked anxiously, 'Who is your Gurudeb? Can you help me? Nobody is willing to help me in this hour of need.'

Wiping Bimala's tears, Trinoyoni praised her Gurudeb and repeated all the lies that she had told Kumkum. Elaborating on how her Gurudeb could help Bimala, Trinoyoni left the lonely, debt-ridden woman with the promise of seeing her near the Manicktola pond the next day.

Halfway home, Trinoyoni remembered that she had forgotten to ask Bimala about her jewellery. Trinoyoni realized that she might have made a mistake assuming that Bimala was still holding on to her jewellery. Bimala was so poor that even a beggar was better off than her. She was worried that if Bimala had already sold off her jewellery, killing her would be useless. Annoyed at her own short-sightedness, Trinoyoni rushed back towards Bimala's house.

As she was about to knock on Bimala's door, the sound of someone digging the soil distracted her. Trinoyoni quickly hid behind the tree in front of her. After a while, she peeped out from behind the tree curiously to find Bimala digging the soil with unbridled enthusiasm. After almost ten minutes of digging, Bimala extracted a white sari from under the ground. It was wrapped and tied together like a sack. Bimala held it to her bosom and hurriedly walked inside her house. Trinoyoni followed her quietly and hid outside her closed door. Since she couldn't see anything, Trinoyoni pressed her ear against the door. The familiar jingling sound of expensive gold bangles brought a grin on Trinoyoni's face. She had no doubt now that Bimala was unwrapping her jewellery from the sack-like sari. Trinoyoni loved and could recognize the sound of jewellery anywhere. The necklaces brushing against the big gold bangles were music to her ears. Trinoyoni tiptoed back home, relieved.

The next morning, Trinoyoni met Bimala and they walked to the pond, crossing the houses, the forests and the gardens, just like she had done with Kumkum. But when she asked Bimala to take a dip in the pond, Bimala refused to leave her jewellery on the steps. Bimala had much more jewellery on her than Kumkum. Even taking off all the jewellery before going to the pond would take a long time. Trinoyoni was nervous that if she lost more time, the sun would be out and someone might spot the women with the jewellery.

'Didi, I insist that you keep all the ornaments here. They will get damaged in the water,' Trinoyoni suggested.

'Oh, don't worry about that, dear sister,' Bimala said, confidently. 'I am a good swimmer and jewellery is my life. Once I had lost a tiny ring in a big pond. I dived under the water and searched for it for almost an hour. Finally, I found it.' Trinoyoni had clearly underestimated Bimala's love for jewellery. It was at par with her own affection for it.

'You didn't get tired under the water?' Trinoyoni asked, appalled.

'No, I can hold my breath for a very long time. I don't get tired at all,' Bimala smiled.

Trinoyoni was in a fix now, as she realized it would be impossible to suffocate Bimala to death. She noticed a big stone near the steps and got an idea.

'Help me pick up this stone, Bimala didi,' she urged.

'But why?' Bimala asked.

'It is a ritual. Since you don't want to take-off your ornaments before entering the water, you need to throw the stone into the water and pray to the water gods to forgive you,' Trinoyoni said, cooking up a story instantly.

Bimala looked confused but she didn't want to offend the water gods. As she bent down to lift the stone, Trinoyoni joined her. Once they had lifted the heavy stone, Trinoyoni deliberately dropped it on Bimala's feet. Bimala lost her balance and fell down on the steps, shrieking in pain as her leg started bleeding.

'Oh, I am so sorry,' Trinoyoni said and sat down holding Bimala's leg. 'Let me see how deep the wound is?' Saying this, Trinoyoni twisted Bimala's leg so badly that she yelped.

'What are you doing? Why are you hurting me?' Bimala said, shocked. She could clearly see the betrayal in Trinoyoni's greedy eyes now and her flared nostrils left no room for doubt as to what she was doing. Trinoyoni quickly tore a part of her own sari and tied Bimala's hands, feet and mouth with it to prevent her from screaming.

'Forgive me, didi! There is no Gurudeb to save you from your miseries. You are leading a painfully cursed life. I will release you from all your oppressions today! There will only be peace!' Trinoyoni laughed breathlessly and started removing the jewellery from Bimala's body.

Bimala was too shocked to react. She could barely move as tears trickled down her cheeks. She only managed to shake her head, begging Trinoyoni to stop. But Trinoyoni was so focussed on robbing the poor woman that she didn't stop to look at her even once. She was absorbed in the jewellery she was holding in her hands. She wanted to hold more.

After removing all of Bimala's jewellery, Trinoyoni carefully placed them on the steps. Next, she dragged the woman to the pond. Bimala couldn't walk nor could she stand up. Trinoyoni knew very well that it would be impossible for Bimala to swim in that condition or hold her breath for long.

Without wasting any more time, Trinoyoni hauled Bimala into the water, but held her close to prevent her from drowning. Trinoyoni was able to touch the bottom of the pond with her feet and so she kept walking till the depth of the water increased. She held Bimala's shoulders tightly with both hands and pushed her head under the water. The poor woman tried her best to get out of the water but she couldn't resist Trinoyoni for too long. When Trinoyoni was sure that Bimala was dead, she removed the cotton cloth from Bimala's mouth and untied her hands and feet. The lifeless body flowed with the water. The bleeding in Bimala's leg had stopped.

Trinoyoni reached the steps and started wrapping the looted jewellery inside the same cotton cloth pieces that she had used to tie Bimala's mouth, hands and feet. Then she waited patiently till she couldn't see the body anymore.

On her way home, Trinoyoni lauded herself for using her presence of mind to deal with the tricky situation with Bimala. As she recalled the fear in Bimala's eyes, Trinoyoni laughed. She was overcome with a sudden sense of power and achievement. Her only regret was that getting rid of Bimala had taken so much time, increasing her risk of getting caught. Trinoyoni knew that she had to plan better for her next kill.

Almost two months after her death, the police found Bimala's body in the Manicktola pond. This too was dismissed as a case of drowning, as nobody could identify the victim.

Trinoyoni sold the stolen jewellery and got paid handsomely by the different jewellery brokers she was connected with. Her past glory as a courtesan allowed her to be free of suspicion, and she began hunting for her next victim.

A Close Shave

A month after Bimala's murder, Trinoyoni killed Sukanya, another woman from the Sonagachi brothel in a similar fashion and dumped her body in the pond. Trinoyoni had made a lot of money from Bimala's jewellery and need not have planned her next crime so soon. But, like a hunter looking for the next prey, Trinoyoni had become addicted to the feeling of holding jewellery and the excitement of having power over others.

However, as she grew older, Trinoyoni realized that she didn't have the strength to kill young women anymore. She was in her forties now, and the years of work had taken a considerable toll on her body. One of her victims had almost overpowered her and Trinoyoni was scared that if she failed even once, the game would be over. As a result, she decided to hire an accomplice for her next crime. But that was not an easy task and Trinoyoni scouted for months to select the perfect partner.

In 1881, after a long search, Trinoyoni met a very poor woman in her neighbourhood who could be a good fit as her assistant—Maya, a strong and loyal woman, almost ten years younger than her. Since Maya was a smooth talker,

Trinoyoni was confident that she wouldn't succumb to pressure if interrogated by the police. Trinoyoni knew that it would be easier to work with her if they lived in the same house. Maya happily accepted Trinoyoni's offer to move in with her, as that would help her save house rent and she would not have to worry about food. In a short span of time, Trinoyoni and Maya developed a sisterly bond. Trinoyoni loved having Maya around because she was kind and caring towards Manik too. However, despite everything, Trinoyoni kept a close watch on Maya to be doubly sure that she had chosen the right accomplice.

Maya was a clever woman too. One day, she caught Trinoyoni searching her belongings and commented, 'If you cannot trust me, we cannot work together, Trinoyoni didi.'

Embarrassed, Trinoyoni replied, 'No, no, I was only looking for some gur. It's Manik's birthday and I thought of making him some paayesh.'

'Oh, you should have told me that, didi. I will make paayesh for Manik today,' Maya said, adding, 'Didi, we are in this together. Even if we fall apart someday, I will never give your name to the police. Please don't distrust me again.'

Trinoyoni nodded and said, 'I, too, will protect your secrets till the last day of my life, Maya.'

∞

Between 1881 and 1883, using the same spiritual guru trick, Trinoyoni and Maya killed three more prostitutes: Kanak Bala, Sabitri and Anupama.

Trinoyoni would lure the women to the pond and

convince them to leave their jewellery on the steps before taking a holy dip. The gullible women would obey her blindly. Once they were in the pond, Maya would pounce on them unannounced and the women would fail to escape from the murderous trap. Finally, they would succumb to the torture and die. Trinoyoni and Maya would collect their loot and leave the pond quietly. The murders had become a cakewalk for them and slowly the duo was no longer afraid of getting caught.

Trinoyoni was rich again. She didn't feel any guilt for the serial killings. Her only concern now was Manik. It was becoming increasingly difficult to plan criminal activities with the adolescent Manik around. Earlier, it had been simpler since Manik could be sent outside or put to sleep. But now, the boy had started asking questions. Trinoyoni had a hunch that he knew something, but she didn't have the courage to ask him anything and humiliate herself. She wanted to keep Manik away from all that she had been doing for him.

One day, without Trinoyoni's knowledge, Manik followed Trinoyoni and Maya to the pond and saw them killing a woman. He was too shocked to react. He returned home and didn't speak to anyone for several days. He would often wake up in the middle of the night weeping.

To cheer him up, Trinoyoni and Maya began pampering Manik by cooking delicious food for him. They tried to teach him the mannerisms of a babu and indulge in babugiri. But Manik was a simple boy who had no interest in the display of vague opulence and wealth. He was more interested in the world around him, especially the social movements and protests against the British rulers that had just started gathering steam. Sometimes, when he used to talk about the news and read the newspaper to Trinoyoni, she was reminded of her friend Rudrapratap. Maybe Manik would become a great samaj sebi like him, Trinoyoni thought. Which is why it was all the more important for her to see that her son got the best of everything.

Manik used to secretly write poems about India's struggle, admiring young men who dared to protest against the injustice meted out to Indians by the British government. However, he was an introvert by nature and never thought of actively getting involved in organized protests. Manik was fond of watching plays too. He had heard about the famous courtesan-turned-stage-actress Nati Binodini and was deeply inspired by her. He wanted to take his mother to watch a play starring the famous Nati Binodini, but could never bring himself to broach the topic with her. It was hard to talk to her after all that he had seen. What was worse was that Manik knew that his mother was indulging in these criminal activities only to earn money and provide for him. His education, the books he bought and the plays he watched; they were all possible thanks to his mother's murderous vocation. Manik was afraid that the police would find out about his mother's wrongdoings one day, but he had no idea how to dissuade her from the world of crime.

Trinoyoni and Maya were geared up for their next victim now, a young woman named Iraboti. Like the others, Iraboti was also from Sonagachi but had moved out of the brothel. She, too, lived in a rented accommodation inside a slum, like the other victims. Trinoyoni had used her charm to convince

Iraboti into meeting the fictitious guru.

On the morning of their meeting, Maya fell severely ill and couldn't accompany Trinoyoni to the Manicktola pond.

'Let's do it another day, didi,' Maya suggested.

'No, you take rest and get some sleep. I'll do it alone. I have done this before and Iraboti is a fragile girl,' Trinoyoni replied. It would be tough, but Trinoyoni was sure that she could do this herself.

Manik, who was listening to the conversation from outside the room, walked in.

'Can I come with you mother?' he asked.

Startled, Trinoyoni said, 'Err...no. I...I have some urgent work. You take care of Maya mashi. I will come back and cook mutton-rice. We haven't had meat in a long time.'

Manik didn't say anything. He just lowered his head. He couldn't bring himself to tell his mother that he was aware of her murderous adventures.

That day, Trinoyoni reached the pond a little late. On the way, she kept thinking about Manik. Why did he want to accompany her? He had never mentioned having any interest in her work before. Had he heard something?

Iraboti was anxiously walking up and down the garden when Trinoyoni reached.

'Oh, didi, I thought you had forgotten about me. I have been waiting for a long time.'

Trinoyoni apologized, 'Sorry sister, I got late. My son is ill. I had to take care of him. Come, let's go.'

It was a hot day and the scorching sun was unbearable. When they reached the pond, Iraboti removed all her jewellery and stocked them on the steps, even before

Trinoyoni could ask her to do so.

'Why did you open your ornaments?' Trinoyoni asked, trying to sound surprised.

'I don't want them to get spoilt in the water,' Iraboti replied.

Trinoyoni nodded and both of them stepped inside the pond for the mandatory holy dip.

After a while, Trinoyoni pressed Iraboti's neck with all her might and pushed her under the water, not letting the woman get up. Iraboti struggled to break free but Trinoyoni kept pushing her down. Suddenly, Trinoyoni felt someone pulling her by the hair from behind. Shocked, she let go of Iraboti and turned around to see a fisherman pulling her away from the water.

In her excitement to kill Iraboti and steal her jewellery, Trinoyoni had forgotten to survey the surroundings. That was Maya's task and Trinoyoni hadn't done it in a long time.

'Leave me, you filthy man! What are you doing?' Trinoyoni shouted.

'First you come out of the water, horrid woman,' he screamed back. Then, the man noticed Iraboti coming out of the water, gasping for breath.

As she reached the shore, the man asked, 'Are you okay, sister?'

Iraboti was shivering in fear and sobbing. 'Thank you for saving my life, dada. I will never be able to repay your debt in my life. This witch wanted to kill me.'

'I came here by accident,' the man said. 'As I was passing by, I heard the sound of water splashing. I thought it was weird because usually nobody comes here at this hour. The splashing was so loud that I came here to check. Then I saw this woman pushing your neck down into the water. I ran to help immediately.'

Iraboti grabbed all her jewellery from the steps. She offered a gold chain to the fisherman but he politely refused. Iraboti folded her hands, lowered her head and thanked him.

'What should we do with this evil woman?' Iraboti asked. 'I assume she must have killed other women by lying to them and trapping them like me. I was lucky, but I don't know if the others were able to escape.'

'You are right,' the fisherman said, still gripping Trinoyoni's right elbow tightly. His eyes scanned her whole body. The sari was clinging on to Trinoyoni's bare body and he could see her skin beneath the sari. Trinoyoni was quick to notice the lust in the fisherman's eyes and she played it to her advantage. She deliberately brushed her body against his hands. The fisherman couldn't take his eyes off Trinoyoni now.

Iraboti noticed the act and told the fisherman, 'You won't be able to do anything with her. She is a cunning woman. She will seduce you and steal all your belongings.'

The fisherman became conscious immediately. 'Don't worry, sister! You go home. I will take this wicked, characterless woman to the police station right now.'

Iraboti looked at Trinoyoni angrily and left as fast as she could. The fisherman dragged Trinoyoni to the police station. When they reached, Ratan Lahiri, an elderly policeman, was on duty.

The fisherman complained, 'I want to report a case of attempted murder near the Manicktola pond. I caught this woman trying to kill another woman. Please arrest her, daroga babu.'

Ratan examined the fisherman from head-to-toe. The fisherman was wearing faded clothes, looked like he belonged to a lower caste and had a pungent body odour.

'Stand away from my desk, you filthy outcaste!' cried Ratan, disgusted with the fisherman's appearance. He sprinkled some water around his desk and murmured some mantra.

Then, he looked at Trinoyoni, who, despite her faded youth and wet clothes, looked very much the naïve and helpless woman.

He wrote down their names and asked, 'What is the matter?'

The poor man narrated the entire episode of how he found Trinoyoni pushing Iraboti under the water and rescued her.

'Where is the woman you saved?' policeman Ratan asked with furrowed eyebrows.

'The poor woman was shivering in fear. I asked her to go home,' replied the fisherman candidly.

Now, Ratan asked Trinoyoni, '*Mohashoya*, is this man speaking the truth?'

As soon as he uttered these words, Trinoyoni started crying.

She said between sobs, 'No, he is lying. I was crossing the pond when he started shouting that I had stolen his fish. When I denied, he pushed me to the pond and I was completely drenched. Then, he dragged me here. Now, he is making up these horrible stories. I am a simple, god-fearing woman, daroga babu.'

Agitated, Ratan warned the fisherman, 'Get out of here before I arrest you!'

'But will you not register my complaint, daroga babu?' the man asked, confused and afraid for his life.

'Complaint? Those big lies? Leave before I arrest you and beat the hell out of you.'

Trinoyoni was pleasantly surprised at Ratan babu's behaviour. He wasn't paying any heed to the fisherman.

'Both of you, leave this place immediately!' Ratan instructed.

Trinoyoni ran out of the police station as fast as she could. When she reached home, Maya and Manik were anxiously waiting for her.

'We cannot do this anymore, didi,' Maya lamented, after hearing Trinoyoni's story.

'We will think of something else, don't worry,' Trinoyoni replied like a seasoned criminal. Then, she proceeded to the kitchen to cook mutton-rice for Manik.

The Return of Daroga Sukumar

Towards the end of 1883, the police discovered the dead bodies of all of Trinoyoni's victims from the pond. But, owing to lack of evidence, they were ready to dismiss the deaths as suicides committed by bankrupt prostitutes. However, before finally declaring it closed, the case of these unknown dead bodies was handed over to Daroga Sukumar Bandopadhyay for a detailed investigation.

When Sukumar studied the case in detail, he didn't get a good feeling. Why would all the women choose the same pond to commit suicide? It didn't look like a mass suicide because from the condition of the dead bodies it was evident that some of the women had drowned much earlier than the others. None of them had drowned on the same day. Sukumar wanted to probe further. However, the doctors ruled out any foul play owing to lack of evidence. Finally, Sukumar had no choice but to accept their verdict that either the women had committed suicide or had drowned accidentally.

On the other hand, Trinoyoni was getting increasingly worried that even though the police had not arrested her on the basis of the fisherman's complaint, Iraboti was still alive and that could be dangerous. She decided to lie low for a while and put all criminal adventures on hold.

Almost after a month, when Trinoyoni thought that the worst was over, Maya came running to her with terrible news.

'Oh, didi! We are doomed,' Maya cried. 'That low woman. Iraboti! I wish we had killed her.'

'What happened?' Trinoyoni asked impatiently.

'Iraboti is talking rubbish about you in Sonagachi. She is telling everyone that you are a fraudster and murderer. She is praising that low-caste fisherman for saving her life and...'

'Why did you stop? And what?' Trinoyoni asked, raising her voice.

'She...she is saying that you are addicted to murdering women. She is calling you a brutal serial killer. She claims that you have killed many women but failed to trap her,' Maya said, panting.

'Who told you all this?' Trinoyoni asked, appalled.

'Everyone in our neighbourhood is talking, didi! We can't live here anymore. They will kill us or hand us over to the police!' Maya said, nervously.

'Don't worry, Maya. No harm will come to you,' Trinoyoni reassured her.

∞

That night, Maya fled from Trinoyoni's house with her belongings and share of the looted jewellery. When Trinoyoni saw her empty room the next morning, she knew that Maya was gone forever. As she was contemplating her next move, someone knocked on her door.

As soon as Trinoyoni opened the door, she froze with fear. Daroga Sukumar was standing at her threshold along with two police constables. His face brought back a series of unpleasant memories of Ram babu's trial and Trinoyoni felt numb.

Sensing her discomfort, Sukumar narrowed his eyes, 'How are you, Trinoyoni Debi? We are meeting after years and I can see that you are leading quite a comfortable life.' He walked inside without waiting for her invitation and looked around as he spoke.

Trinoyoni was back in her senses and knew that she was in trouble. She tried her best to stay calm and replied with folded hands, 'How can I help you, daroga babu?'

'I would like to ask you some questions,' Sukumar replied coldly.

'Sure, and please eat lunch at my house today,' Trinoyoni said in a sugar-coated voice, welcoming the policemen into her house. The constables were very happy when she mentioned food, but Sukumar was not impressed.

'We haven't come here to eat,' Sukumar fumed. 'Do you know a woman called Iraboti Debi?'

Trinoyoni pretended to think for a while and then replied, 'Yes, she is my friend from the Sonagachi brothel.'

'Good,' said Sukumar. 'You will have to come with me to the police station.'

Trinoyoni didn't know what to say. Her heart was beating faster and she regretted not leaving the house when Maya had raised an alarm the previous evening. Her hands were cold with fear as she imagined the story Iraboti might have narrated to Daroga Sukumar!

Trinoyoni decided to quietly follow the police out of the house. On their way out, Sukumar saw Manik standing by the door.

'Who is this young man?' Sukumar asked.

'My son, Manik,' Trinoyoni replied.

'Your son? Oh, Ram babu's son! He is quite grown up now, I see!' remarked Sukumar.

Trinoyoni lowered her head and stepped out of the house as Manik looked on.

When they reached the police station, Sukumar walked up to Ratan Lahiri's desk along with Trinoyoni. The elderly policeman, who had earlier interacted with Trinoyoni and the fisherman, stood up nervously.

'Is this the woman against whom the fisherman wanted to lodge a complaint?' Sukumar asked him.

Ratan Lahiri nodded anxiously.

'Why didn't you write the complaint, Ratan babu?' Sukumar admonished him.

'He...he was lying, daroga babu,' Ratan said, fumbling.

'You are answerable to the magistrate now,' Sukumar warned Ratan.

Trinoyoni and Ratan quietly followed Sukumar to the magistrate's office. Ratan was too scared to speak. Trinoyoni took a deep breath and tried her best to stay calm.

The Magistrate thundered, 'How can you take such an important accusation lightly, Mr Lahiri? I will dismiss you from service if this *raur* is found guilty. I want a thorough investigation on this case. I am immediately suspending you from service for your carelessness in handling a vital criminal case.'

Ratan kept his head lowered and didn't utter a word. When Sukumar informed him that the magistrate had decided to send the case to trial, Ratan's heart sank! He was aware that the only way he could save himself was by proving Trinoyoni Debi's innocence. Trinoyoni was clever enough to understand that too. This was a boon for her and she didn't need to spend any money to defend herself during the trial. Ratan had taken it upon himself to investigate the matter in detail, bribe people, prepare false witnesses and present the case in such a manner that Trinoyoni was declared not guilty.

When the case was tried in court, Ratan did his best to save his career and, by extension, Trinoyoni's life. Iraboti's claims were dismissed in court and, she was established as an opportunist—a characterless woman who wanted to rob the decent Trinoyoni Debi of her money. The lower caste fisherman's testimony was completely disregarded. Ratan had bribed the lawyer to establish that the fisherman and Iraboti had had a clandestine affair and were out to loot a hapless prostitute who was saving every bit of her money to give her only son a decent upbringing. Trinoyoni, too, acted exceedingly well as the distraught mother.

After hearing out all the witnesses and on the basis of the evidence provided by Ratan, the jury voted in favour of Trinoyoni and declared her not guilty. Daroga Sukumar was extremely disappointed with the verdict. He glared at Trinoyoni leaving the courthouse; she had managed to escape his clutches for a second time.

As soon as Trinoyoni returned home from the court, she began contemplating her next move. She knew that even though the court had given her a clean chit, the scandal could ruin her life. Almost everyone in Sonagachi had heard the spiritual guru story. News had spread that she was a conwoman and serial killer.

Trinoyoni knew that she was no longer safe in her rented house. People would bang on her door late at night, hurl abuses at her and even throw stones inside her house. One day, a stone hit Manik's forehead, injuring him badly. The attacks were getting more and more serious by the day. Fearing for her son's safety she finally decided to move.

Rajlakshmi's Mysterious Death

When Trinoyoni left home with Manik in search of a new rented house, she had no idea where she was headed. She inquired in the neighbourhoods in the vicinity, but nobody was willing to rent out a house to a single woman.

After walking for a long time, Trinoyoni and Manik reached the Chitpur area in North Calcutta. Tired, they sat down by the road and began eating the flattened rice and curd that Trinoyoni had packed. Suddenly, a beggar appeared from nowhere and started crying loudly. He sat down near Trinoyoni's feet and pleaded for a morsel of food. Trinoyoni felt sympathetic towards the beggar and offered her food to him. Manik was rather astonished to see his mother's act of kindness. It was the first time he had seen her helping someone from whom she had nothing to gain! Moved by this gesture, Manik offered his share of the food to the beggar too. The beggar grabbed the food and finished it within seconds. Then, he sat down beside Trinoyoni and asked, 'You look like a rich woman. Why are you sitting on the road?'

Trinoyoni merely smiled at him but Manik said, 'We are looking for a place to stay.'

Trinoyoni was surprised to see Manik talk to the beggar

with such urgency. Before she could say anything, the beggar replied, 'Oh, I know a good place. Come with me.'

A tad surprised, Trinoyoni and Manik followed the beggar through the narrow lanes of Chitpur till they reached a double-storey house in the Panchu Dhobani Gali. Trinoyoni paid the beggar some money and thanked him. Delighted, he showed them the main gate of the house and left. The area felt safe and Trinoyoni manged to rent a small room. The adjacent rooms boarded several other tenants—all women. Luckily for Trinoyoni, her notorious reputation had not spread to this narrow lane yet.

True to her amiable nature, Trinoyoni befriended the other women in the house within days. She became good friends with Parul Bala. A sharp and clever girl, Parul was much younger than Trinoyoni.

'I am always looking for avenues to earn more money, didi,' Parul admitted to Trinoyoni while discussing their miseries one evening. 'But I don't know what to do!'

Trinoyoni could read Parul's mind very well. Parul's bearing and tongue were very similar to that of Maya. Trinoyoni knew she had found her next accomplice. 'I have some ideas, but I am not sure if you would be willing to help me execute my plans.'

'Just tell me and I will do it,' Parul replied promptly.

'Even if the means to earn the money are not fair?' Trinoyoni asked, testing her.

Parul started laughing wickedly. 'After leading a prostitute's life for so many years, do you really think I care about what is fair and what isn't?'

Trinoyoni smirked and posed another question to

Parul. 'Then tell me, who is the wealthiest person in this house?'

'I know what you mean,' Parul grinned. 'I love her jewellery. Come, I will introduce you to Rajlakshmi didi.'

Soon, Trinoyoni, Rajlakshmi and Parul were inseparable. They would often spend time together, chatting, visiting the nearby market, cooking and discussing the many men in their lives.

Rajlakshmi would say, 'Trinoyoni didi, you are the elder sister I never had.'

Trinoyoni became so friendly with Rajlakshmi that she knew every nook and corner of the wealthy woman's room. It didn't take much time for her to figure out where Rajlakshmi stored her jewellery.

'Does your babu treat you well, Rajlakshmi?' asked Trinoyoni.

Rajlakshmi's shoulders drooped and she sighed. 'Well, the richest babu left last year. He used to pay me handsomely. Now, I am not a mistress anymore. I sleep with anyone who has money. How about you, didi?'

Trinoyoni shook her head. 'I don't sleep with anyone anymore. I am old now, and don't have many takers. Besides, by the grace of God, I have enough money to sail me through the rest of my life.'

'Oh, but you are not that old. You look so beautiful, Trinoyoni didi. I am sure if you get a good man, he will not let you go,' Rajlakshmi remarked. Parul started giggling.

The bond between the women grew deeper over the next few months. Trinoyoni and Parul were inching closer to their goal.

Even after eight months, Daroga Sukumar had not been able to forget the case of the dead bodies retrieved from the Manicktola pond. Though Sukumar got busy investigating other criminal cases, the discomfort of not finding credible closure to the case kept haunting him. Though the doctors had ruled out any foul play, Sukumar was not convinced.

Moreover, Sukumar couldn't get over the story that Iraboti had narrated in the court about how Trinoyoni had lured her to the pond using a made-up spiritual guru as the trap. He failed to understand why the jury had given a clean chit to Trinoyoni despite such strong accusations against her of attempt to murder. Why did the court discard the statements of both Iraboti and the fisherman?

Sukumar's mind travelled back to Ram's trial too. He remembered his first meeting with Trinoyoni while investigating the robbery–murder case against Ram, her pimp and partner. Her sharp eyes and diplomatic responses to his questions had convinced Sukumar that Trinoyoni was not an innocent, helpless woman. Instead, she was, perhaps, the most dangerous woman he had met in his entire life. Sukumar couldn't rule out the possibility that the innocent-looking Trinoyoni Debi was perhaps a serial killer on the prowl!

One morning, in August 1884, when Sukumar reached the police station after a week's leave, he received a notice from his senior to investigate the brutal murder of a courtesan whose dead body had been found inside her own home in Panchu Dhobani Gali in North Calcutta's Chitpur area.

'When did this happen?' Sukumar asked his subordinate while leafing through the case file.

'While you were away, daroga babu. Five days back, on 10 August 1884,' the subordinate replied.

'Tell me whatever you know about the case,' Sukumar instructed.

'This woman of low birth and character, called Rajlakshmi, who lived in a house in Panchu Dhobani Gali, was suffocated to death in the early hours of the morning. The assailant stole all her jewellery and valuables and killed her. Several policemen have visited the house and spoken to the tenants, but none of them have been able to crack the case yet. Some of our colleagues are still there, working on the case.'

Curious and alarmed, Sukumar decided to rush to the crime site. When he reached, he saw five policemen stationed inside the house, busy in an intense discussion.

Sukumar remarked, 'Sorry to interrupt your interesting session, gentlemen. I wanted to know how I can assist you in this critical case.'

One policeman replied, 'We have thoroughly investigated and interrogated everyone in this house, daroga babu. However, we haven't found the culprit yet. There isn't much to do in this case, it seems.' The policeman yawned and resumed chatting with his colleagues.

Sukumar replied with a dash of sarcasm, 'Oh, I see that you and your team have already done everything. There's hardly anything left for me to contribute.'

The policemen stared at him, wondering what to say.

Sukumar finally asked, 'Who informed you about this murder?'

Chandi Nath Gangopadhyay, the policeman leading the case in Sukumar's absence replied, 'This news was first reported to the police about a week ago by Shiboproshad Mukhopadhyay, the deceased Rajlakshmi Debi's landlord. He owns this house, but he doesn't live here.'

'Where does he stay?' asked Sukumar.

'He stays in a bigger house, a little far from this place.'

'Okay, what did he tell you?' asked Sukumar.

'He was informed about the murder by a tenant in this house. The woman told him that Rajlakshmi was lying dead in her room. Shiboproshad babu reached the crime scene immediately. When he saw Rajlakshmi's body, he realized that she had been killed. That's when he reported the matter to us,' Chandi Nath concluded.

'Who was the first to arrive on scene out of all of you?' asked Sukumar.

'I came here first, daroga babu,' replied Chandi Nath. 'When I reached, Rajlakshmi's room was wide open and she was lying on the floor. The moment I saw her, I knew she was dead. We sent the body for post-mortem immediately.'

'And who in this house was the first to see the dead body?'

Chandi Nath was starting to find this daroga irksome. As a policeman, he felt insulted that his rigorousness was being doubted.

A tad miffed, he responded, 'A woman named Bhabani Kumari. She is also a tenant here, and a prostitute, like the other women. She found it odd that Rajlakshmi didn't join her and the others for the early morning bath that day. So, she went to her room to fetch her. After calling out to Rajlakshmi many times, when she didn't get a response, Bhabani entered the room. She found Rajkumari lying awkwardly on the floor. Scared, she screamed for help. When the other tenants reached Rajlakshmi's room and saw her dead, they immediately called the landlord.'

Sukumar listened attentively and asked, 'Only women reside in this house?'

Surprised at the detective's question, policeman Chandi Nath whispered, 'Yes, daroga babu! This is a whore house. In the evenings, you will find men in every room. I have been told that some of the women even entertain two to three men at the same time.'

'Okay, enough,' scoffed Sukumar. 'I'd like to see the room now.'

As Sukumar entered Rajlakshmi's room and looked around, he assumed that the killer must have strangled the woman the previous night and sneaked out.

Sukumar asked, 'When you entered the room, in what position did you find the dead body? Was she lying on the floor or on the bed?'

Chandi Nath replied, 'She was lying on the mattress.'

'Did you find any injury marks on the victim's body?'

'Not injury marks as such,' answered Chandi Nath. 'But the doctors found deep marks all around her neck. They look like finger impressions and marks of sharp nails. Like I said, she was strangled to death.'

'What else does the coroner's report say?' Sukumar asked, curiously.

Chandi Nath's face turned pale as he narrated the post-mortem report. He now realized why this daroga was so successful and thorough. Chandi Nath immediately knew that he did not have the mettle to be a daroga like Sukumar. Before narrating the report, he muttered a silent prayer.

'Rajlakshmi Debi was killed brutally. The murderer was no less than a monster. He sat upright on her chest, gripped her neck tightly with both hands and pressed them down with all his might. She was choked to death by a beastly man!'

Tapping his own chin with his fingers, Sukumar asked, 'But how can the doctors be so sure that the killer was sitting on her chest?'

Chandi Nath lowered his voice and stepped closer to Sukumar, 'I feel horrible sharing this piece of information, daroga babu. The tender bones on Rajlakshmi's chest and her ribs were either broken or distorted. The murderer applied so much pressure on the fragile woman that it broke her bones.' He shivered at the ghastly scene he envisioned.

'What a barbaric creature,' thought Sukumar as he visualized the gruesome image of the murder in his mind.

There was a moment of silence. Then, Sukumar asked, 'Could you retrieve anything from Rajlakshmi's room that can count as evidence?'

'We found several things, actually. Two bronze plates with marks of curd, parched rice and jaggery. Perhaps Rajlakshmi and her assailant were eating together when he struck her,' Chandi Nath commented.

'How can you be sure that the culprit is a man?' asked Sukumar.

Chandi Nath laughed nervously, 'How can a woman commit a murder of this nature? How can she have the strength to break Rajalakshmi's bones? Besides, did you look at the women in this house, daroga babu? They are all petite and frail.'

Sukumar didn't respond to Chandi Nath's remark. Instead, he asked, 'Did the coroner find the remains of these food items in the victim's stomach?'

'Yes,' said Chandi Nath. 'And she had been poisoned.'

'What kind of poison?' asked Sukumar curiously. *What was the need for poison when the person was being strangled?* He wondered if this was indeed a crime of passion as the other policemen had assumed.

'I don't remember exactly, daroga babu. But I have noted it down in the report,' Chandi Nath replied, a little embarrassed.

'Okay. Did you find anything strange in Rajlakshmi Debi's room?' asked Sukumar.

'Not in her room but we noticed that Rajlakshmi wasn't wearing any jewellery. We don't know if her killer stole the ornaments, or someone removed them from her dead body. However, it is evident that her jewellery was stolen. She was not a widow and it was strange that she wasn't even wearing earrings,' Chandi Nath explained. Now, the remaining policemen around were interested in how Daroga Sukumar was operating. The yawns and discussions were replaced by looks of amazement.

'How about her belongings? Anything missing from there?' asked Sukumar.

'The women here said that she was the richest prostitute in this house. But her trunk and almirah had no valuables. Her sealed mud-pot containing coins was broken. The thief took all her money and jewellery.'

'You can refer to her as the victim or the deceased. You don't need to keep repeating that she was a prostitute. We already know that,' Sukumar ordered Chandi Nath, glaring at him.

Chandi Nath nodded with a surprised look on his face.

'Anyway, have you made a list of her jewellery?' asked Sukumar.

'We are trying to compile it by talking to the other prostitutes—I mean women in this house. Usually, women remember and identify jewellery very well, even if it is not their own,' replied Chandi Nath.

Sukumar asked, 'Did you interrogate the men who had visited Rajlakshmi that night?'

Chandi Nath said, 'Yes. There was only one man, who left early in the evening. I have spoken to him already. He is a zamindar from Purulia and has recently shifted to Calcutta. She didn't have any other visitors, according to the other tenants.'

'Did anyone else from the house meet her?' asked Sukumar.

'Two tenants who were Rajlakshmi's friends visited her. They live on the upper floor. We spoke to all the ten women who live in this house individually. None of them apart from those two met Rajlakshmi on the evening before her death.'

Sukumar asked, 'What about the main gate of this house? I didn't see any security guard outside. That means the tenants operate the gate. Who was the last person to lock the gate?'

'A woman called Kamini claims to have locked the gate at midnight after her customer left. But nobody knows if a tenant opened the door from inside the house after that.'

Sukumar asked, 'Did Kamini Debi open the door in the morning too?'

Chandi Nath replied, 'No, daroga babu! Bhabani, the woman who saw Rajlakshmi dead, opened the door to go to the landlord's house.'

'It's possible that one of the tenants killed Rajlakshmi and didn't leave the house at night. But the person must have gone out the next morning to hide the stolen jewellery at least!' opined Sukumar. 'This also rules out the customers from our suspect list. But I am not sure yet if that's the right thing to do.'

Chandi Nath excitedly added, 'Daroga babu, I have checked with every male member believed to have been present in the house that evening. All their alibis are genuine. We have visited their houses and they have been interrogated several times at the police station.'

'Okay, so nothing suspicious about the women present in the house either? Then who committed the murder? A ghost?' Sukumar asked angrily.

'We did suspect one woman initially. She has just been here for four months. We have been following her movements closely. But she appears to be clean,' replied Chandi Nath.

'What's so special about this woman, if I may ask?' Sukumar commented sarcastically.

'Nothing special. In fact, she is nice and caring. However, there are rumours that she was accused of killing several prostitutes and stealing their jewellery. She made up some story about a spiritual guru who blessed women with jewellery and absolved them of their sins. Her case went to court too, based on another prostitute woman's report. But the jury found her innocent. None of us believe this story though. Apparently, the plaintiff was a greedy woman who was trying to blackmail poor Trinoyoni for money,' Chandi Nath said confidently.

Sukumar's jaw dropped as he heard this familiar story.

'What was the name of this mystery woman again?' he asked impatiently.

'Trinoyoni Debi,' replied Chandi Nath. 'The tenants here address her as Trinoyoni didi.'

Sukumar crossed his arms, 'Are you sure this is the same Trinoyoni Debi who faced the Alipore sessions court, being accused of murder and was released as innocent?'

'Yes, I have heard that she is the same Trinoyoni,' replied Chandi Nath.

Anxiously, Sukumar lit a cigar. Then, he said, 'If this is the same Trinoyoni, let me tell you that we are dealing with a very dangerous woman here. She will not think twice before committing another murder. Murder is merely a chore for her, like washing dishes or cooking a meal! If we have to save the residents of this house, this serial killer must be arrested and punished at the earliest.'

'But, daroga babu!' Chandi Nath exclaimed in a confused tone.

Sukumar ignored him. Even though he didn't have any facts to substantiate his claim, Sukumar knew that Trinoyoni had killed Rajlakshmi. She was dangerous and capable of committing the most heinous of crimes. This was his opportunity to catch her once and for all. After having failed twice, Sukumar was now a man possessed.

Sukumar contended, 'You have no idea what a charmer

this woman is! I convicted her and remanded her to police custody on account of murder charges a few months back at the Alipore court. It was an open and shut case. There was no way she could get out. She didn't even have the money to afford a lawyer. There was an eye-witness who saw her trying to forcibly drown a woman in a pond. But she got away! You know how?'

All the policemen stared blankly at Sukumar.

'Trinoyoni Debi was saved by a policeman who was trying to save his job! Because of his misjudgement, nobody registered the complaint against Trinoyoni lodged by a poor fisherman, the sole witness in that attempted murder. Instead, the seasoned policeman—Ratan Lahiri—did everything possible to save this wretched woman and keep his job!

A few years back, when I was new to the detective department, I had arrested her in connection with another case. But the lucky fraudster had gotten away that time too! Her partner Ram Chandra Dutta was given the capital punishment. If she is the same woman, I will recognize her instantly.' Sukumar gnashed his teeth and punched a wall in frustration after remembering his failure.

'Would you like to meet her now, daroga babu?' another policeman asked.

Sukumar put out his cigar and mused, 'No. Not yet. You continue to watch her. She shouldn't know about my involvement in this case at all.'

'Are you sure, daroga babu? Trinoyoni Debi is very cooperative. She answered everything we asked her. We have searched her room thoroughly. She hardly has any belongings. Besides, her behaviour is extremely good. She serves tea, tobacco and hookah to all of us. Whenever we visit the house, she offers us paan and even food at times,' the policeman added gleefully.

'She stands out from the other women, right?' asked Sukumar.

All the policemen nodded.

Chandi Nath added, 'She is so interested in the investigation! When we look around the house, the other women are never there. But Trinoyoni is always present, sticking with us like a part of our team. In fact, my team members are very impressed with her. She pampers everyone and they enjoy it.'

'There you are! That's her nature! Tell me now, how did you learn about her past?' asked Sukumar.

'A few days back, a policeman was passing by this house and recognized Trinoyoni. When he heard about Rajlakshmi's murder, he asked her to confess to the crime. When I asked why he was harassing her, the policeman told us about her alleged involvement in the other murders! After that, we interrogated her many times and scanned every corner of her room. We found absolutely nothing. She is innocent, daroga babu. I apologize, but I must say that just because she was accused earlier, doesn't mean she is guilty of this too,' Chandi Nath said assertively. He looked suspiciously at the daroga. Ever since Trinoyoni's name had been mentioned, Sukumar had a manic look in his eyes.

Sukumar placed a hand on Chandi Nath's shoulder and said, 'Listen, young man, Trinoyoni Debi fooled the magistrate, the judge and even the jury! You and I are lesser mortals. It is a near impossible task to get her to speak the truth. She can stoop to any level to free herself. Trust me! I have been fooled twice. I don't want to mess it up the third time.'

'Then what do you think we should do with her now?' another policeman asked.

'We have to get her to admit to the crime. Otherwise, regardless of the evidence we collect, she will get away.' Sukumar rubbed his bruised fist and remembered how Trinoyoni had escaped the last time.

'We have tried everything,' Chandi Nath cried.

'Did you search her room properly?'

One of the constables replied, 'We have left no stone unturned in searching her room, daroga babu. We found nothing except her bare essential belongings and minimal jewellery.'

Sukumar said in a serious tone, 'I have studied the pattern of her crimes closely. She usually has a partner to execute her criminal activities. If we can find that companion, half the battle will be won! Who is her closest friend in this house?'

'There is a woman named Parul who is very loyal to Trinoyoni,' Chandi Nath replied.

Daroga Sukumar's eyes lit up, 'Take Parul into custody without Trinoyoni's knowledge. Scare her till she admits to the crime! Where is Trinoyoni's son? Does he live here too?'

Chandi Nath replied, 'Yes, a teenager. He has gone out with his mother. Should I call her back? A policeman is escorting them. So, at least she will not be able to escape.'

'No, that's not required. She will not even try to escape. Just remove Parul from this house before Trinoyoni returns,'

Sukumar ordered, a plan slowly taking shape in his clever mind.

'Yes, daroga babu, I will do so immediately,' Chandi Nath replied anxiously.

'I will leave now. Meet me at the police station in the afternoon. I have a plan,' Sukumar instructed the group of policemen before leaving.

Trapping the Serial Killer

Later that afternoon, policeman Chandi Nath Gangopadhyay and Daroga Sukumar Bandopadhyay had a long discussion at the police station. Chandi Nath was entrusted with the crucial task of speaking with all the tenants in Rajlakshmi's house in Trinoyoni's absence.

Sukumar advised, 'Be careful, young man! Trinoyoni Debi is a master of deception and fraud. She is an enchantress who will catch you unawares if you talk to her for too long! You must keep the interactions crisp and short.'

At around seven o' clock, as Daroga Sukumar entered Rajlakshmi's house, he saw that all the tenants had gathered in the inner courtyard of the house. Several policemen were present too. Then, Sukumar spotted Trinoyoni, sitting quietly at one end of the courtyard, her hands and legs tied with rope.

Sukumar hurriedly walked towards the nearest policeman and asked, 'Isn't she Trinoyoni Debi?'

The policeman answered in the affirmative.

'Why have you tied her up?' Sukumar asked, raising his voice.

'She has killed Rajlakshmi Debi, a tenant of this house,' replied the policeman.

Appearing perplexed, Sukumar contended, 'Nonsense! Do you have any evidence?'

'She is a dangerous serial killer, daroga babu! She has killed many others in the past. We don't have any evidence yet, but we cannot let her roam about freely. She is a threat to all the others in the house!'

'How do you know about her past?' Sukumar asked feigning ignorance.

Policeman Chandi Nath came forward now. With a miffed expression, he asked, 'Why, daroga babu? Don't you remember that you once arrested this woman in an attempt to murder case?'

'What the hell is going on here?' Sukumar shouted to attract everyone's attention.

'Are you a bunch of foolish policemen? Just because I arrested this poor Brahmin woman in the past, you concluded that she is a murderer? Do you have any idea about the kind of life she has led or the adversities that she has had to face? I made a mistake of suspecting and arresting this innocent lady. It was a false case lodged by a lower caste fisherman to trap her and seize her belongings. I was wrong and I deeply regret hurting her. When the jury found her innocent, who am I to label her a thief? My friends, don't you have faith in the judicial system?' Sukumar admonished all the policemen present for their ineptitude.

After patiently hearing out Sukumar, Chandi Nath commented, 'You are certain, then, that Trinoyoni is innocent?'

Sukumar nodded vigorously.

'Then please enlighten us, daroga babu. Who robbed and

killed Rajlakshmi? She was the wealthiest prostitute in this house,' said Chandi Nath.

In response to the Chandi Nath's plea, Sukumar declared confidently, 'I have a fair idea who it might be. But before that, please release this poor woman. You have harassed her enough!'

With a grim face, Chandi Nath instructed a constable to untie Trinoyoni's hands and feet. Though initially shocked at his statement, Trinoyoni was relieved and thanked Sukumar with folded hands. Then, she sat down beside him.

Sukumar glanced at her from the corner of his eye and cleared his throat. Then, he announced, 'I would like to speak to the tenants of this house individually please.'

Chandi Nath immediately added, 'But we have already spoken to everyone.'

With a raised eyebrow, Sukumar asked, 'Well, I haven't. Do you mind?'

'Not at all, daroga babu. Please go ahead,' Chandi Nath snarled with sarcasm.

'Give me the statements of all the tenants please,' Sukumar urged.

Chandi Nath handed him some papers and Sukumar tore them off immediately. 'I am destroying these prejudiced statements given by the tenants. They are trash and have no value for me. I will restart the interrogations.'

Trinoyoni's face lit up as she saw Sukumar tearing off the statements given by the tenants against her.

Sukumar proceeded towards the corner of the courtyard and Trinoyoni, who had been sitting next to him all along, began following him.

On the way, a constable stopped her. 'You cannot go there till all the tenants have given their statements.' She nodded nervously and walked towards a pillar, right behind where Sukumar was sitting. Sukumar smiled wryly. He was happy that she had taken the bait.

One by one, the tenants of the house walked up to Daroga Sukumar and recounted their experiences from the night before Rajlakshmi's murder. The first tenant to give her statement was Manjulika Debi, a woman in her forties and the inhabitant of the corner room on the ground floor.

Sukumar asked her, 'What do you have to say about Rajlakshmi Debi's murder? Is there anyone that you suspect?'

Manjulika Debi spoke slowly and softly. She started, 'Rajlakshmi was a jovial girl and we all loved her. She was so pretty and wore such beautiful jewellery! She used to be very popular. But, off late, she wasn't getting too many customers. I...' She paused.

Sukumar sensed her hesitation and prompted, 'Go on, please.'

Manjulika continued, 'I am embarrassed to say this but Rajlakshmi was having an affair with a young boy...a teenager. Her customers didn't like the attention she was paying to this boy. Perhaps that's why they stopped visiting her.'

Sukumar asked curiously, 'Who is this boy? You know him?'

Manjulika said, 'Yes, everyone in this house knows him. He is Manik, our new sister Trinoyoni's son. He is friendly with all the women in this house. He enters their rooms often. I don't even see him studying nowadays. He used to be a bright boy, I have heard.'

Then, lowering her voice, Manjulika added, 'I have seen him indulging in drinks and meat, sitting in Rajlakshmi's room. Now tell me daroga babu, Trinoyoni Debi is not rich. How does Manik get so much money to splurge? The night before Rajlakshmi's death, I saw Manik entering her room and closing the door after him. Trinoyoni didn't know that they were in love. When I heard weird sounds coming from the room that night, I thought they were enjoying physical intimacy. I didn't talk about it as I didn't want to cause a scandal.'

Sukumar nodded and stroked his chin, 'Okay, you may leave now. Who is next?'

Trinoyoni was speechless when she heard Manjulika's statement! She had never expected accusations against Manik, and she did not know what to do about them. Her heart was beating out of her chest and Trinoyoni started sweating.

After Manjulika, it was Bhabani's turn to give her statement to Sukumar. Bhabani was the first person to have spotted Rajlakshmi's body.

She told Sukumar, 'That night, when my babu was leaving, I went to see him off to the main gate of the house. I was surprised to find the gate open at that odd hour as it was well past midnight. I closed the door and went back to my room.'

'Did you see anyone leave the house?' asked Sukumar.

Bhabani shook her head and was sent back after a few other questions. Trinoyoni was relieved that Bhabani didn't mention Manik.

The third tenant was a seventeen-year-old girl named

Prafulla. Trinoyoni knew that Manik liked Prafulla but couldn't muster up the courage to talk to her. Prafulla, on the other hand, was a thorough professional. She was the mistress of a zamindar's son and proudly proclaimed herself to be the queen of the house. She was not conventionally beautiful, but she had an irresistible charm and an hourglass figure.

Prafulla rested against the pillar as she gave her statement, 'The morning Rajlakshmi didi died, I woke up very early, as my babu wanted to leave. As I walked to the main gate, I saw Manik entering the house. He looked tired and distressed.'

Sukumar enquired, 'Didn't you ask him what happened?'

Prafulla replied, 'Usually he stares at me all the time. But that day, he lowered his head and sheepishly walked into his mother's room before I could utter a word.' She shrugged as her statement was noted down and went back to her room.

Similarly, the other tenants came forward and gave their statements to Sukumar. All of them had found Manik's behaviour odd that night. One of them even said that, from her balcony, she had seen Manik and Rajlakshmi getting physically intimate. Rajlakshmi's window had been open and the tenant had clearly seen a bare-bodied Manik sitting on top of Rajlakshmi.

'Why didn't you report this to the police earlier?' Sukumar asked indignantly.

'I...I thought they were doing something else. But now that I think about it, I am sure that Manik was pressing Rajlakshmi's neck and choking her,' the lady murmured apologetically.

Parul couldn't be interviewed because, as per Sukumar's instructions, she had already been taken into police custody.

The last tenant to give a statement was Charubala Debi. Charubala, one of the more senior and trusted residents of the house, stated, 'That night, I stepped out of my room to drink some water, as the jug in my room was empty. I had to cross Rajlakshmi's room to go to the kitchen. As I passed by her room, I heard moaning sounds and assumed that she was with a babu. Though, I must say that the sound was very peculiar. It was not the usual sound women make while indulging in sexual activity. When I was walking back from the kitchen with my jug full of water, I saw Manik exiting Rajlakshmi's room. I was rather shocked! He was panting and walking hurriedly towards the main door with a big bag in his hand. I called out to him but he didn't look back. Instead, he ran out of the house. I guess he was carrying the stolen jewellery in that bag.'

Nobody asked Trinoyoni anything nor did they try to blame her. She stood like a statue, helpless and unable to save her son. She let her tears drop silently. In the meantime, Manik returned home. He was surprised to see everyone in the courtyard, along with so many policemen. Nobody had noticed him entering through the main gate and he stood behind the crowd of people quietly.

Finally, Sukumar said, 'Now that we have spoken to everyone, it is clear that Manik is the culprit. He stole Rajlakshmi's jewellery and killed her. Let's arrest him.' Chandi Nath nodded gravely and accepted Sukumar's deduction.

Manik was shocked. He couldn't find his voice and just kept staring at his mother. The policemen noticed him now. Two constables quickly got hold of Manik and began dragging him out of the house.

Manik stopped in front of his mother and sounded in control, 'Don't worry, Ma, I will be fine. You know that I am not a criminal and that's all that matters to me!'

Trinoyoni was startled at her son's mature statement. He hadn't given her away despite being aware of her criminal pursuits.

Sukumar slapped Manik across the face, 'Shut up, you liar! Where is the jewellery? I will beat the hell out of you. I cannot wait to welcome you to prison!'

Seeing her son getting hit broke Trinoyoni. She came between Sukumar and the door he was exiting from. 'One minute, daroga babu,' Trinoyoni pleaded. 'Can I please speak to you in private, for a moment? I beg of you!'

The daroga nodded and led Trinoyoni to the drawing room on the ground floor. The tenants and policemen stared at them as the two walked away.

'Should we move this boy to jail in the meantime, daroga babu?' asked Chandi Nath, sniggering.

With folded hands and tearful eyes, Trinoyoni looked at Sukumar, pleading for mercy.

'Wait till I come back,' Sukumar ordered before he retreated to the drawing room with Trinoyoni.

'Daroga babu, I swear on Ma Durga, my child is innocent. They are all lying. Please don't ruin his life!' she cried as she threw herself at his feet.

Sukumar took a step back to avoid Trinoyoni and curtly replied, 'That's not possible at all. Why would they speak against him?'

Trinoyoni fumbled. She had no answer for this sudden hostility of her fellow tenants towards Manik. 'I really don't know! He is a saintly boy. He has never even hurt a fly. You can ask Parul. She knows. I cannot find Parul today. But she can vouch for him.'

Daroga Sukumar narrowed his eyes, 'How does Parul know so much?'

Trinoyoni went quiet.

The detective asked again, 'Come on, tell me. How does your friend Parul know that Manik is innocent? Does she also know who killed Rajlakshmi?'

Trinoyoni sighed. The game was up, and she had been defeated. But she had to save Manik in any way possible. Shivering, she confessed, 'Yes, Parul knows everything because she helped me rob and kill our dear friend Rajlakshmi.'

Trinoyoni's confession did not alter Sukumar's expressions. He knew that he had to weigh his words well before speaking; else, the serial killer would escape again.

Sukumar spat and said irritably, 'Huh! You are just protecting your son and taking the blame, like any good mother would!'

Trinoyoni appealed, 'No, no! Please believe me! I am the criminal. Manik is innocent.' It was an odd reversal from the previous times Trinoyoni and Daroga Sukumar had been together in a room.

Sukumar claimed, 'You cannot fool me, Trinoyoni Debi! Had your son been innocent, you would have announced that in front of everyone. We wouldn't need this private conversation then!'

'If that is what you think, daroga babu, I will confess my crime in front of everyone so that you believe me,' Trinoyoni walked out of the room and proceeded to the courtyard, where everyone was waiting. Sukumar followed her, trying his best to suppress his excitement.

Trinoyoni announced to the almost full courtyard, 'My son Manik is innocent. He has not killed anyone. I appeal to all of you to please take back your statements. I killed Rajlakshmi with my own hands. Ask Parul if you don't believe me. She knows everything.'

There was pin-drop silence. Some of the tenants exchanged quick, terrified glances. Bhabani, who was standing closest to Trinoyoni, moved away from her with other women following suit. Soon, Trinoyoni was standing by herself, and the rest of the women had congregated at the other end of the courtyard.

'Why did you kill Rajlakshmi Debi?' asked Sukumar.

'I am a very poor woman. I needed money to take care of my son. Rajlakshmi had a lot of jewellery—all expensive and unique,' she said blankly. 'I wanted to steal all her jewellery for my personal gain. The plan never involved killing her. I just wanted her to faint. The death was purely an accident. Oh, please believe me, I didn't want her to die.'

'Accident? Are you sure?' asked Sukumar.

'When all efforts to make her faint failed, I had no option but to resort to murder,' Trinoyoni replied, her face devoid of any emotion. Manik stared at his mother, stunned. Everyone in the house was shocked at her candid confession.

'What was the plan, exactly?' Sukumar asked sternly. 'Did Manik help you?'

'No, Daroga babu. Manik had no clue. After I came to this house, Parul became my best friend. We learnt that

Rajlakshmi had a lot of jewellery. Just like me, Parul needed money too. Together, we hatched a plan to rob Rajlakshmi,' Trinoyoni responded.

Sukumar stood silently, waiting for Trinoyoni to complete her confession. He almost had her in his grasp. He could not afford any more slip-ups now. He remained patient and limited himself to simple and short questions.

'What about the drug? How did you drug her?' he asked.

'I grew up in a village, you see,' Trinoyoni continued. 'So, I used a natural drug. I travelled to the outskirts of the city to pluck seeds of the dhutura flower. As you must be aware, debauched people often smoke dhutura to get high. All I had to do was grind the dhutura seeds, mix them in a drink and serve it to Rajlakshmi. I was confident that she would doze off soon after consuming the drink. That would allow Parul and me to steal her jewellery without any hassles.'

'What happened next?' asked Sukumar.

'I had the mixture ready but I wasn't getting an opportunity to serve it to Rajlakshmi as a drink because she refused to consume alcohol. Finally, I had to change my plan and buy sweets.'

'What happened after that?' Chandi Nath asked anxiously.

'Parul called Rajlakshmi to come to my room and we chatted for a long time, discussing love, life and relationships. I was about to serve the sweets to her but Parul signalled with her eyes advising me against it. That's why it is important to have an accomplice for a crime. Had Rajlakshmi fainted in my room, it would have been difficult for us to move her out.'

Trinoyoni rubbed her moist eyes as she remembered how she and Parul had trapped Rajlakshmi on that cursed night.

'I am very sleepy,' Trinoyoni said, yawning. 'Let's chat again tomorrow.'

'Come on, didi, don't act so old. Let's walk Rajlakshmi didi to her room at least,' coaxed Parul.

The three women climbed up the stairs and reached the threshold of Rajlakshmi's room.

'Listen to my tragic love story before you go to sleep, didi,' insisted Parul and dragged Trinoyoni inside Rajlakshmi's room.

Once inside, they sat down on a mattress on the floor. It was the same mattress on which Rajlakshmi's dead body had been found.

'The problem is, if I stay up till late, I feel hungry,' complained Trinoyoni. 'Do you have anything to eat Rajlakshmi? Else, I will go back to my room!'

'I have parched rice and curd. Would you like to have that?' offered Rajlakshmi.

Trinoyini agreed. Rajlakshmi fetched three plates but Parul said, 'Two plates will suffice. I will eat very little and I can share from Trinoyoni didi's plate.'

Taking this opportunity, Trinoyoni added, 'Why don't you get the sweets from my room Parul? That'll go well with this food.'

Parul smiled and ran out. Within minutes, she was back with the dhutura-mixed sweets from Trinoyoni's room. Trinoyoni kept the fresh sweets in her plate and served the dhutura-mixed ones to Rajlakshmi.

'I am not feeling well, didi,' Rajlakshmi complained

within minutes of consuming the food. She was tipsy but still in her senses.

∞

'Did she lose consciousness finally?' asked Sukumar, pulling Trinoyoni back from her trance.

'She didn't', Trinoyoni replied. 'I didn't have any other option but to push her to the floor. I jumped on her chest and gripped her neck with both hands. Parul pressed her legs down tightly so she wouldn't be able to move. I strangled her till I was sure she was dead!'

Manik fell on his knees, covered his face with his hands and started crying as he heard his mother narrate the horrific tale. He had thought that she had stopped her criminal activities after the last time when she had almost been caught. He still found it hard to believe that his mother was capable of such things.

'Parul and I removed all the jewellery from her body and also stole all other valuables from her room. Then, we slipped back into our rooms quietly,' said Trinoyoni, like a cold-blooded murderer.

All the tenants and the policemen looked at her, astounded.

Sukumar was apprehensive that Trinoyoni might pull one of her old tricks to escape going to prison, like she had done in the past. Almost the entire confession was out now. He just required evidence. Sukumar was sweating in anticipation.

He quickly asked, 'Where is the jewellery that you claim to have stolen? Unless we get that, we cannot believe you.

Maybe you are making up stories to save your son.'

'Come with me,' Trinoyoni said. There was a strange calmness within her, as if she knew how everything was going to proceed now, and no matter what anyone tried, those things were not going to change.

Sukumar and the others followed her to her room.

She opened her almirah and took out a box of sweets. 'Send this for the doctor's examination. You will find traces of dhutura in these. I haven't seen Parul today. If she was here, she would confirm that I am telling the truth.'

Sukumar looked at the sweets and asked one of the constables to send them for examination. 'Where are the ornaments?' he asked.

'Here, in my room,' replied Trinoyoni, surprising everyone.

'You are lying! We have searched every corner of your room multiple times. How is it possible that we didn't find the jewellery?' Chandi Nath queried.

'It's all in my almirah,' Trinoyoni replied. 'I will show you.'

Saying this, Trinoyoni pulled the almirah forward and walked behind it. She tapped the back of the almirah and pulled open a chamber, like a secret locker, which was otherwise not visible.

Sukumar looked furiously at Chandi Nath, who was staring at Trinoyoni in amazement. This is why patience was needed till the end. Trinoyoni was too clever for most people.

Trinoyoni dug her hand inside the locker and pulled out a large bag, overflowing with all kinds of gems and gold jewellery.

'You would have never found the jewellery if I hadn't opened the locker for you, daroga babu,' Trinoyoni said, bitterly. 'This secret compartment is built in my almirah in such a way that nobody can find it unless they know the design of this almirah.'

The police searched the locker thoroughly. They found traces of dhutura and a lot of cash inside it.

'The cash is mine. Please leave it,' Trinoyoni requested.

'Everything here is stolen, you wretch,' a tenant lashed out from behind the curtain of policemen.

'She would have killed us all. Please take her away,' cried another tenant.

'Trinoyoni Debi, we are arresting you for robbing and murdering your neighbour Rajlakshmi Debi,' proclaimed Sukumar.

'Just tell me one last thing, daroga babu. I am curious to know,' Trinoyoni asked as the policemen tied her hands. Despite the finality of it all, she surprised herself by crying.

'What?' asked Sukumar.

'Where is my friend Parul? She was my partner in crime!'

'Parul Bala is a state witness now. She has agreed to speak against you in court,' came Sukumar's reply.

The tears stopped suddenly. The sequence of events started making sense to Trinoyoni and she started laughing hysterically. 'Oh, so all this while you were playing hide and seek with me, daroga babu? I am so foolish that I stepped into your trap! Last time, when I killed so many women in the pond, you couldn't punish me. But this time, you succeeded. Congratulations!'

Sukumar replied calmly, 'You have cheated too many people and committed too many crimes. It all ends here.'

Looking at the tenants, Trinoyoni screamed, 'I must

applaud you all for your brilliant acting!' Enraged, she continued, 'Good that Parul is on your side, daroga babu! At least she will not be executed. Had I been in her place, I would have done the same thing.'

Manik came running to his mother, crying.

'You knew everything, didn't you, my son? Why didn't you tell me that you knew your mother is a criminal?' Trinoyoni howled. She couldn't control her tears anymore. She hugged him tightly.

Manik didn't say anything. Trinoyoni was taken into police custody.

Daroga Sukumar Bandopadhyay presented Trinoyoni Debi's case to the Magistrate, who reviewed it meticulously and sent it to the Calcutta High Court for trial.

The Execution

In September 1884, the lawyers presented the judge and the special jury with ample evidence and a line of witnesses, all of whom claimed that forty-four-year-old Trinoyoni Debi was guilty of murder. The main witness was Parul Bala, Trinoyoni's accomplice who had turned into a *rajshakkhi* and consented to testify against her. In lieu, the Magistrate had agreed to grant pardon to Parul in the Empress vs Rajlakshmi Raur murder case.

In her statement, Parul said, 'Trinoyoni Debi took good care of me because she knew that I was in dire need of money and would do anything to survive. However, I had no idea that she was trapping me into committing a ghastly crime! I was so deeply influenced by her that I lost my sense of judgement. I couldn't differentiate between right and wrong. I became greedy for money and agreed to assist her in robbing Rajlakshmi Debi. But I had a change of heart and did not finally participate in the robbery or the murder of Rajlakshmi Debi. I have never indulged in any criminal activities with Trinoyoni Debi.'

Trinoyoni glanced at Parul and smiled to herself.

'We had dinner with Rajlakshmi didi that day after which

I returned to my room. Later that night, I saw Trinoyoni didi going towards Rajlakshmi didi's room with a big bag. Afterwards, the accused confessed to me that she had robbed and killed an inebriated Rajlakshmi. She also threatened to kill me if I told anybody anything about the murder,' Parul lied.

Before concluding her statement, Parul made another shocking revelation. She stated, 'Further, the accused admitted to me that before moving into the rented house at Panchu Dhobani Gali, she had murdered at least six women in the last three years by drowning them in a pond near Manicktola and robbing them of their jewellery and valuables. She committed some of the murders alone and, in the others, she had an accomplice.'

However, despite the claims made by Parul and other witnesses, Trinoyoni refused to plead guilty. She kept repeating, 'I have not killed anyone.' She had accepted defeat, but something in her was still fighting and refusing to go down and die quietly.

During the trial, the prosecution showed evidence proving that fingernail marks had been found on the victim's neck. The statements from Parul and a few other tenants convinced the jury that before Rajlakshmi's murder, Trinoyoni's fingernails were long. Sukumar reckoned that when she gripped the victim's neck, her nails must have broken. He further stated that when the police checked, they found that her nails were short and broken.

The prosecution also mentioned that the accused Trinoyoni was stronger than the fragile Rajlakshmi, who had a thin frame. This had enabled the accused to kill the victim easily.

The Execution

As per the law, every statement of the witnesses had to be corroborated. Based on all the evidence provided, the postmortem report, and statements of the investigation officers and police surgeons, the arguments of the prosecution as well as the statement of the witnesses, the special jury gave its verdict.

Before spelling out the verdict, Trinoyoni was asked if she wanted to say anything in her defence. But she merely repeated the same sentence over and over again, 'I have not committed any crime. I have not killed anybody.'

The special jury found Trinoyoni guilty of theft and murder. The verdict stated that her greed to enhance her own wealth had made her extremely ruthless. She had committed the most horrific crime possible and, therefore, deserved the worst possible punishment.

On 4 September 1884, Trinoyoni was given the capital punishment: 'To be hanged till death.'

Trinoyoni was calm and expressionless when she heard the judgement.

She was taken back to her prison cell in the Calcutta Alipore Jail, where Daroga Sukumar visited her one last time.

Since the trial started, Sukumar had started feeling uneasy. Even though he knew she was guilty and deserved to be punished, he felt sorry for her. While she had been remorseless, Sukumar knew that the world around Trinoyoni Debi had let her down. When he saw her sitting in one corner of her cell, crying uncontrollably, Sukumar felt remorseful and apologized to her.

'Forgive me for I have sinned! I am responsible for

the execution of a Hindu Brahmin woman,' Sukumar told Trinoyoni with folded hands.

She barely looked at him or spoke. When Sukumar was about to leave, Trinoyoni politely made her last request to the detective. 'Please enquire after my dear son Manik sometimes, daroga babu.'

Daroga Sukumar was taken aback at her motherly concern. Instead of celebrating his success after capturing a notorious serial killer, the ace detective walked out of Trinoyoni's prison cell with a heavy heart.

While serving jail time, Trinoyoni sent a petition to the then governor of Bengal, requesting him to free an innocent woman like her from police custody. However, the governor refused to interfere with the judgement delivered by the Calcutta High Court.

After a few days, Trinoyoni Debi was executed in Calcutta by the British, per the laws of the land. Other than her son Manik, nobody grieved her death.

Afterword

The character of Trinoyoni Debi is inspired from the true story of Troilokya Tarini Debi, one of India's earliest known serial killers. Referred to as 'Troylucko Raur' (Troilokya—the prostitute) in nineteenth-century Calcutta police records, her story illustrates how a simple village girl's relentless struggle for survival turned her into a prostitute, a fraudster and, finally, a serial killer

Despite the restrictions of a rigid caste system, Troilokya's zest for life filled her with the motivation to create her own path in a world that was cruel to women. She fought to survive despite the burdens of widows in the nineteenth century, with patriarchal structures that considered the death of the husband as the end of a woman's life too. Daroga Priyanath Mukhopadhyay, the police detective who succeeded in nabbing Troilokya for the notorious crimes she had committed, considered her to be the most dangerous woman he had ever met.

Historians and criminal psychology experts are divided in opinion as to whether Troilokya was a serial killer in the true sense of the term or just a dangerous assassin. While there is reason to believe that Troilokya didn't commit the murders merely for psychological thrill, she was a mission-oriented devious slayer who meticulously planned her crimes.

We learn about Troilokya's life and crimes primarily from the writings of Priyanath Mukhopadhyay through a series of periodicals called *Darogar Doptor*. Not much is known about Troilokya's childhood, except that she was born a Kulin Brahmin and grew up in a small village in Bengal. Nevertheless, she created a sensation in the world of crime and had mastered the art of cajoling law enforcement officers and getting away with her dangerous lawbreaking acts.

Though Troilokya has earned the name of India's 'Jack the Ripper', she was executed at the order of the British government in 1884, several years before the world had even heard of Jack the Ripper! While Jack the Ripper terrorized the streets of London between August and November 1888, Troilokya reached her criminal peak in the 1870s and was arrested in the early 1880s, after which she was inmate number 8979 at the Alipore Jail in Calcutta.

Perhaps the biggest similarity between Troilokya and Jack the Ripper is that their victims were all poor women prostitutes. From her background and police reports, it is evident that Troilokya's key motive for murdering these women was to steal their jewellery and valuables. Jack the Ripper, on the other hand, brutally tortured most of his victims before killing them.

Unlike Troilokya, who killed prostitutes who had been her friends and acquaintances, it is believed that Jack the Ripper, also known as the 'White Chapel Murderer', was not acquainted with any of his victims.

In his book *The Wicked City*, historian Sumanta Banerjee

states, 'Jack the Ripper was a homicidal maniac'. According to Banerjee, explanations about Jack's behaviour continue to be 'mired in modern sociological controversies', as to whether the motive was some 'deep-rooted psychological perversion' or 'an evangelical zeal' (to get rid of prostitutes).* On the other hand, research has shown that Troilokya was a cunning opportunist. As author and historian Anindita Ghosh says, she was a serial killer, proficient in 'robbing and drowning her victims mercilessly for private gain.'**

From Priyanath Mukhopadhyay's accounts in *Darogar Doptor,* especially in the story 'Paharey Meye', we learn of the humane side of Troilokya. She had lost her heart twice to the men she loved. Her love for her adopted son knew no bounds and, eventually, she owned up to her crimes to save her son.

About Troilokya's criminal pursuits, Banerjee writes, 'It is a real-life story of a picaresque adventuress, which towers over fictitious accounts of similar women like Daniel Defoe's "Moll Flanders" or John Cleland's "Fanny Hill."'

Troilokya Debi's notoriety spread across Bengal and the whole of India much after her death.

---

*Banerjee, Sumanta, *The Wicked City: Crime and Punishment in Colonial Calcutta*, Orient BlackSwan, Delhi, 2009.
**Ghosh, Anindita, *Claiming the City: Protest, Crime, and Scandals in Colonial Calcutta (c. 1860–1920)*, Oxford University Press, Delhi, 2016.

Further Reading and References

1. Mukhopadhyay, Priyanath, *Darogar Daptar,* Vol. 1, 2, 3, Punascha, Kolkata, 2021.
2. Banerjee, Sumanta, *The Wicked City: Crime and Punishment in Colonial Calcutta*, Orient Blackswan, Delhi, 2009.
3. Ghosh, Anindita, *Claiming the City: Protest, Crime, and Scandals in Colonial Calcutta (c. 1860–1920)*, Oxford University Press, Delhi, 2016.
4. Banerjee, Sumanta, *Dangerous Outcaste: The Prostitute in Nineteenth-Century Bengal*, Seagull Books, Kolkata, 2019.
5. Fifth Criminal Sessions Report, Empress vs Troylucko Raur (published in *The Statesman* and *Friend of India*, 4 September 1884).
6. The Murder & Mayhem Walk, organized by Heritage Walk Calcutta in December 2018.

Glossary

aanchal	the part of the sari that goes over the shoulder
alta	red dye
ashtamangala	a post-wedding ritual where the bride and groom visit and spend a couple of days at the bride's house
atithi	guest
bashor raat	wedding night celebrations usually attended by young relatives and friends of the newly-wed couple
beshya	courtesan
beshya polli	colony of courtesans
bhadralok	gentleman/genteel
biyer piri	a wooden platform on which the bride and groom sit
bonedi bari	a traditional Bengali aristocratic house
borondala	a welcome kit of sorts used to welcome

	the groom by the women of the bride's family. Contains, among other things, kumkum, incense sticks, a lit clay lamp, turmeric, sweets and rice
botua	handbag
bou-bhat	a ceremony or celebration hosted by the groom's family usually one or two days after the wedding that guests from both sides attend
babugiri	partaking in activities in order to network with the upper classes of Bengali society
dana kata pori	a fairy without wings
dhaak	percussion instrument
dhutura	*Datura stramonium* or Devil's Trumpet
dudh-chire	flattened rice and milk
gaaye holud	a ceremony where the groom and bride are bathed in turmeric. Also known as the haldi ceremony in other parts India
haats	fairs
jamai babu	son-in-law
kanya pon	money paid by the groom to the bride's family for wedding expenses
kumkum	red turmeric powder used for making the distinctive Hindu bridal mark on the forehead

Glossary

mangsho bhaat	mutton curry and rice
mohor	gold coins
neel chaash	indigo farming
pagdi	headgear
panjabi	kurta
payal	anklet
phool shojya	first night after the wedding
shakha-pola-nowa	bangles worn by married women
purohit	priest
rajshakkhi	state's witness
raur	derogatory word for courtesan
samaj sebi	social worker
shishya	student
shondhya-arati	evening prayers
thakur dalaan	a public courtyard, often with pillars and verandahs reflecting influences of European architecture
topor	traditional Bengali wedding headgear
uthon	inner courtyard of a house
yajna	prayer before holy fire

Acknowledgements

Thank you, dear reader, for investing your time in my book. Hope you enjoyed reading it.

A huge thank you to the following amazing people who made this book possible:

The team at Rupa Publications, for their incredible help and support. I would especially like to express my deepest gratitude to my editors, Rudra Sharma and Akshay Rana, for their insightful suggestions and brilliant edits to make the manuscript better. Thank you both so much! Thanks to Oorja Mishra and the copyediting team for their prompt response and support at all times.

The Book Bakers literary agency for all the help, encouragement and guidance. This book wouldn't have been possible without Suhail Mathur, my fabulous literary agent. When I discussed the idea of the book with Suhail, he immediately asked me to send a synopsis and within a month, I signed my first commissioned assignment with Rupa Publications!

The Immersive Trails, a historical tour agency co-founded by Dr Tathagata Neogi. I got the idea of writing this book after attending their popular Murder & Mayhem walking tour in Kolkata. I am truly grateful to Dr Neogi and his team for their eagerness to help me and for the invaluable research inputs and recommended readings.

Mr Anjum Rajabali, for the constant guidance and inspiration, and for encouraging me to always focus on the key character's feelings at any given point in the story. Thank you!

Mr Boman Irani, for making me an integral part of the Spiralbound family, for inspiring hundreds of writers like me to not give up during the pandemic and for a million other reasons. Thank you for being an angel in disguise!

My husband, Sagnik Ghosh, for encouraging me to attend the Murder & Mayhem walk, and for continuously buying books and digging up relevant articles to help with my research.

My friends, Pranish Basu and Sikharendra Datta, for sharing useful information on Troilokya and lesser-known criminals of nineteenth-century India.

My wonderful family and friends for being my pillar of strength and source of sustenance.

My teachers from school, college and university—I will always be grateful to each one of you for the knowledge and self-belief that I have gained over the years.

Finally, thank you, God—for everything!